American Daydream

A Collective Work of Psychic Fiction

Curated and Edited by J. Martin Strangeweather

For my enemies,

because this work could not have been created without them.

1.

A majority of the viewers watching *Let's Make a Deal* at home are either middle-aged females or males over sixty. You can tell by the advertisements. The viewers at home wish they could be on the game show themselves. They wish they were the chosen ones, handpicked by none other than Wayne Brady himself to go up on stage and try their luck at a game, any game, but especially a chance to play for the Big Deal. Sometimes the viewers at home wish they had the game show host's job, or even better, the announcer's, Jonathan Mangum, he barely does anything, or better yet, Tiffany Coyne's. Simply to point at things and smile. She's already won the game of life. Many of the female viewers wish they could actually *be* Tiffany Coyne.

One host, unthreateningly black, plus one announcer, excruciatingly white, plus one blonde model who tries her best not to act better than the contestants, multiplied by the prospect of winning cash and prizes, equals thirty minutes of earthly paradise. Their careers consist of nothing more than staying fit, looking good, and not embarrassing themselves too much in public. The viewers at home assume they each have a personal fitness trainer, a team of makeup artists, and a publicist. Most of the viewers at home can't even afford a gym membership.

"And now, here's your host—it's Wayne Brady!" says the announcer, sounding overly excited, looking wholesome as latticed apple pie. Wasn't he involved in some sort of scandal a while back?

"Okay, let's do what we do here," says the host, looking stylish as always in his gray suit sans necktie, sporting a collared metallic blue shirt with the top button unbuttoned. Wasn't he also involved in some sort of scandal a while back? "Who wants to make a deal?" The studio audience clamors, everyone vying to be noticed. "You there, dude in the chicken costume. Come here, chicken man. Come on down and talk to me."

A white male who appears to be in his forties makes his way to the stage, high-fiving other members of the studio audience along the way. "I love you, Wayne!" he shouts, wrapping his wings around the host and squeezing him tight.

"I know you do, chicken man. I know."

"No, I mean I really love you! I'm your biggest fan! I watch you religiously!"

"You're making me feel weird now, chicken man. Come on," says the host, prying himself away from the contestant.

Cat Gray, the show's award-winning keyboardist, presses down on a key which makes the sound effect of a chicken, *buh-*

cack! Wasn't he involved in some sort of scandal a while back, too? Weren't they all?

"Nice to meet you, Dan," says Wayne.

"Oh my *bleep*-ing god! How did you *bleep*-ing know my mother-*bleep*-ing name?!"

"Calm down, chicken man. I just read it off your nametag."

Chicken man blushes and buries his face in his wing feathers.

"Aw, don't feel bad," says Wayne, putting his arm around chicken man. "Tell you what—I'm gonna give you five hundred dollars for making you feel bad."

Chicken man's face lights up.

"Now, you can take this five hundred dollars, or you can have what's inside Tiffany's cute little box." The double entendre is never lost on viewers at home under the age of fifty. "Whatever you don't take," says Wayne, "I'm gonna give to . . ." The camera pans across the studio audience. Out of all the hopefuls shouting and flailing about for attention, one gentleman in a powder blue tuxedo is sitting with his legs crossed, calm and quiet. "You, blue tuxedo guy."

The gentleman in the powder blue tuxedo gets up and walks to the stage, where Wayne Brady offers to shake his hand. The gentleman in the powder blue tuxedo pushes Wayne's hand aside and rubs his shiny bald head, "For good luck," he says.

"Well, okay then," says the host, laughing it off. "So, your nametag says Mr. Mentacity. That's not your real name, is it?"

"It'll do for now," he says.

"Are you supposed to be dressed up as a nerdy teenager going to the prom?"

"What do you mean?" says Mr. Mentacity. "This is how I normally look."

"Oh, sorry. My bad," says Wayne.

The viewers at home can't tell if the contestant in the powder blue tuxedo is being serious. The viewers at home judge him instantaneously, assigning him to a panoply of prefabricated categories that make him relatable to their experience and expectations of someone with his particular outward appearance, constructing another fictional character in the story of their lives. The viewers at home aren't conscious of doing this, and they couldn't stop themselves even if they wanted. Their assessment of him is harsh enough to let them forget about their own flaws for a few minutes: Fat slob, late forties, possibly early fifties. A dwindling wisp of grizzled hair struggles to maintain its foothold on the forepart of his otherwise sweaty bald pate, and prescription glasses frame his bloodshot eyes in thick black squares. His powder blue tuxedo looks three sizes too small and it's blossomed with umber coffee stains, as though he dug it out of a Goodwill bin, or a dumpster.

"All right, chicken man, what's it gonna be, the money or the small box?"

Chicken man Dan looks to the studio audience for advice. He doesn't want to take full responsibility for making the wrong choice.

"I'm going to take the money, Wayne."

"He's taking the money!" says Wayne. A majority of the audience disapproves. They think chicken man chickened out. It's weird how we get worked up over the failures and successes of contestants on these shows, virtual strangers, yet their wins are somehow our wins. Their losses are ours, too. Chicken man waves around the five hundred dollars as if it were a million. "Okay, chicken man," says Wayne, "go on back to your seat."

Cat Gray plays a short tune that ends with *buh-cack!*

"All right, Mr. Mentacity, here's the deal," says Wayne. "I'm gonna give you what's in Tiffany Coyne's small box," and he pulls five $100 bills from his pocket, "or you can take this five hundred dollars."

"Make it five thousand and you have yourself a deal," says Mr. Mentacity.

Wayne Brady chuckles, along with the studio audience. "Sorry, man, that's not how it works. But good try, though."

The studio audience begins shouting their opinions. Mr. Mentacity turns around and faces them. "Please be quiet. I don't need any help from you people." The studio audience looks stunned.

"I'll go with the box, Wayne."

"He's going for the small box!" The studio audience is silent. The studio audience is never silent. Even the viewers at home are feeling uncomfortable. "Tiffany, show us what's in the box."

Tiffany Coyne lifts up the box, revealing a pair of earrings. "You've won designer jewelry!" says the announcer. "These dazzling white gold earrings feature an elegant seashell design set with brilliant round cut diamonds, from Cartier's J&M Collection. This deal is worth two thousand dollars!" The studio audience goes back to acting like the studio audience, clapping and hooting wildly.

"Do you perchance have a special lady in your life, Mr. Mentacity?" The viewers at home notice that sometimes Wayne talks like he's from the ghetto and other times he uses words such as *perchance*.

"What makes you think I like people?"

"Tell you what," says Wayne, "you can take home those earrings which are worth two thousand dollars, or you can take what's behind Curtain Number Three."

Mr. Mentacity considers his options while the audience tries to persuade him.

"Now it could be something good," says Wayne, "or it could be a Zonk."

"Is it a Zonk?" asks Mr. Mentacity, staring intensely into Wayne's eyes.

"Uh, no," says Wayne, sounding somewhat spacey. "It's not a Zonk." The viewers at home weren't aware the contestants could ask that. "So what's it gonna be?" says Wayne.

"Before I make my decision, perhaps you should tell me what's behind Curtain Number Three."

"There's a foosball table behind Curtain Number Three," says Wayne. The viewers at home don't understand. Have the rules changed? They feel disoriented. Approximately a third of them wonder if they're experiencing a bad side effect of their medication.

Mr. Mentacity looks disappointed. "Do you have anything better, Wayne? Maybe something I could drive."

The floor producer, a skinny bald man nicknamed the Money Fairy, runs up on stage and whispers something in Wayne's ear. "More *Let's Make A Deal* right after this," says Wayne, and the program cuts to a commercial for Zoloft, followed by a commercial for Paxil, followed by a commercial for Cialis.

"Welcome back to the show," says Mr. Mentacity. "Today's Big Deal is worth over twenty-five thousand dollars, but right now, who wants to make a deal?" Mr. Mentacity scans the studio audience. "You, the handsome gentleman in the blue tux," says Mr. Mentacity, and the camera cuts to Mr. Mentacity sitting in the studio audience. He points to himself, acting surprised. The camera cuts to the keyboardist, and there's Mr. Mentacity standing behind the keyboard, playing a clumsy rendition of *Thus Spoke*

Zarathustra. The camera pans over to the announcer, but it's Mr. Mentacity again, standing in Jonathan Mangum's place, winking at us.

The disembodied voice of Mr. Mentacity speaks to us from inside our own heads, *"Everyone's a winner here—the cast, the producers, the directors, the equipment operators, the studio audience, the advertisers, even you, the viewers at home."*

"Let's skip all these formalities and go straight to the Big Deal," says Mr. Mentacity, standing center stage.

"Don't go away, folks," says Mr. Mentacity, standing in the back row of the studio audience, all of whom look just as confused as the viewers at home. "We've got the Big Deal of the Day coming up right after these messages." The segment ends with a shot of Mr. Mentacity standing by the three curtains, waiting to show us the Big Deal.

— J. Martin Strangeweather

2.

Two families stand at their respective podiums. They are not facing each other. They are facing the camera. They are facing off with America.

The game is *Family Double Dare*. The set is a rainbow purgatory of garish colors: electric pink and lightning teal and banana yellow and burnt sienna. The teams are red and blue. The host and contestants are white. This is a rerun of the show's final episode, which originally aired on February 6, 1993.

The Red Team introduces themselves as the Gladwell Family. The marquee above their podium reads "Gladwell" against a backdrop of Nickelodeon's iconic green slime. All four of them have moppy blond hair, the parents and their two boys, and they're all wearing red jumpsuits provided by the studio. The father looks like he sells used cars. The host, Marc Summers, always looks like he just farted in church. His features are reptilian, topped with hair like a puffy brown Brillo pad. Wearing a pink blazer and white Reeboks, he ambles over to his banana-yellow podium.

"I understand you enjoy watching movies at home together and going fishing," he says, referencing a card in his hand.

"That's true, Marc," says the father, sweating nervously.

"Eggbert here has autism," says the mother, gesturing proudly to the youngest mop-haired son.

Eggbert grins, fidgeting with his hands. "I've been alive for nine and a half years already."

The boppy music in the background gets boppier. Boppy music has been playing the whole time. The music is like: *bom, bom, bom, bunna buh-baow!*

The Blue Team introduces themselves as HYPNO. The marquee above their podium reads "HYPNO" in iridescent letters that are continuously changing shape. There is only one person in this family, which seems to contradict a fundamental rule of *Family Double Dare*. He is alarmingly tall, at least seven feet, and completely hairless. He doesn't even have eyebrows. His eyes don't blink, and they seem perhaps incapable of closing. It is surprising that the studio has a powder blue jumpsuit tall enough to fit him. Marc Summers minces over optimistically.

"I'm looking at your interests here on my reference card, HYPNO family, and it's just a bunch of weird symbols."

"That's true, Marc," says the man. "I have hypnotism," he says, gesturing to the son he doesn't have.

"We usually go for nuclear family units on this show. Do you have a wife, and, maybe, two children?"

"Don't worry about it," says Mr. HYPNO.

"I won't worry about it," says Marc, returning to his banana-yellow podium. Holding a clutch of index cards in his manicured talons, he begins to read off the first question but is interrupted by the HYPNO family.

"One moment, Marc," says the hairless man. He calls out to the autistic Gladwell boy. "Eggbert, you're on my team now." Eggbert goes and stands next to the man on the HYPNO team. Marc and the Gladwell family nod in earnest approval. Mr. HYPNO has helped them understand the necessity of this event. Eggbert seems excited by the change in perspective.

"Our first question is for the HYPNO family," says Marc. "For ten dollars, HYPNO family: What is the capital of Utah?"

Eggbert and the hairless man confer briefly, then face forward again. Eggbert speaks up. "Salt Lake City."

"That is correct!" says Marc. The audience applauds and the scoreboard under HYPNO now reads "10."

"Eggbert," says the hairless man, "you did very well with that question."

Eggbert beams. "I know all the state capitals! Alabama's is Montgomery, Alaska's is Juneau, Arizona's is Phoenix, Arkansas' is Little Rock—

"That skill will not be useful for you in the workforce," says the hairless man. "But you'll be all right."

"Okay," says Eggbert.

"Does it bother you that your family introduces you as autistic?" asks the hairless man.

"Sort of," says Eggbert.

"Our next question is for the Gladwell family," says Marc. "For ten dollars: Which president is pictured on the twenty-dollar bill?"

The Gladwell family confers. They are not sure, so they choose to pass the question to the other team. "Dare," says the bubbly mother.

"Okay, HYPNO family, this question is now worth twenty dollars. Which president is pictured on the twenty-dollar bill?"

"Wait," says the hairless man, turning to the Gladwell family. "You seriously don't know the answer? You see his portrait almost every damned day."

The bubbly mother frowns. Marc Summers continues smiling his practiced smile full of promises, noticing neither the profanity nor the digression, hardly aware of anything more than cue cards and camera angles.

"It's a simple question that any citizen of the United States should know," says the hairless man. "Eggbert, Double Dare your family. I want them to feel shame."

"Double Dare," says Eggbert.

"Okay, Gladwell family. For forty dollars, do you have an answer, or would you like to take a Physical Challenge?" says Marc.

"Physical Challenge," says the father.

"He chooses the labor of the body," says Mr. HYPNO, shaking his head. "Shameful." He snaps his fingers, summoning a bucket of popcorn and a couch from which he and Eggbert can watch

Eggbert's family make asses of themselves. Eggbert claps his hands excitedly.

"Say, Eggbert," says the hairless man, "why did your parents name you Eggbert? Why would they do that to you?"

"I'm not sure," says Eggbert. "Maybe they thought it was funny." He looks over at his parents. "We're from Alaska. The capital of Alaska is Juneau," twiddling a lock of his moppish hair. "It gets really cold there. Hockey's our favorite sport, next to dog mushing. I like hockey more, but mom and dad won't let me play because they say I might get hurt."

Marc leads the Gladwell family to the center of the stage. At one end of the stage there are twenty-four kiddie pools arranged in four rows of six, full of oatmeal, and at the other end is a funnel that looks like a basset hound's head. Marc Summers explains how the family will have to fish through the oatmeal for hidden Ziplocs of pig blood and empty them into the funnel, where the blood will splash gratuitously onto the floor in an allegory for capitalism.

"This isn't normally what you make the players do," says the neurotypical Gladwell son.

"You made your choice when you stepped onto this stage," says the hairless man. "Your brother is with me now. Your country is against you. Your society has failed you."

"What?" says the neurotypical son.

"Audience, cheer them on!" ejaculates Marc. "On your mark . . . get set . . . goooo!"

The timer reads thirty seconds, but it does not count down. After eight hours of hard and degrading labor, the family is covered in cold oatmeal and hot pig's blood and is no closer to earning forty dollars. A steady cascade of blood sluices down the basset hound funnel's chin. The floor is a cesspool, a terrible slurry, and the Gladwells can no longer make the circuit between the kiddie pools and the funnel without slipping. They are repeatedly injured. There does not seem to be a winning condition to the game. Eggbert laughs and laughs—the physical challenges are his favorite part of the show—and eventually indicates to Mr. HYPNO that he has tired of the spectacle. The hairless man snaps his fingers and the timer buzzes.

"Ohhh, I'm sorry, Gladwell family, you didn't quite make it in time!" says Marc, who has been in a sort of suspended animation during the Physical Challenge until this point.

"Make it where?" says the father, livid and panting, showing all of his teeth. "What was the goal?" The mother is making the type of involuntary, rhythmic growling noise that you make when you've cried all you can cry, and the neurotypical son is on his hands and knees, retching in front of Marc's podium. They are herded back to their stations.

"Forty dollars goes to team HYPNO!" says Marc. "And they receive our next question." Marc pauses and puts down his index cards, staring directly at the camera. "Why did Eggbert's parents name him Eggbert?"

The Gladwell family is agape at this seeming breach in the objectivity of the trivia round. Mr. HYPNO has a serious look on his face. He turns to the audience and says, "That's a good question, Marc." He scowls at Eggbert's parents. "Dare."

"For twenty dollars now, Gladwell family . . ."

"This is stupid," says the father. "This isn't the game we signed up for."

"This is the game your lifestyle created," says Mr. HYPNO.

". . . why did you name him *Eggbert?*" says Marc.

The mother and father confer in a hushed tone. It's almost as if they're hiding something. The neurotypical son, covered in blood, is facing away from the audience and beating his fists on his knees.

"Double Dare," says the mother, and she bursts into tears. The father's face is bright red.

"Only Mr. and Mrs. Gladwell possess the words to answer this simple question, Marc," says the hairless man. "Therefore Eggbert and I will have to solve it with our bodies. We take the Physical Challenge."

"The HYPNO family has chosen to take the Physical Challenge!" reiterates Marc.

Mr. HYPNO and Eggbert are called to the center of the stage, which has been mopped clean of the previous catastrophe. The stage is Clorox spotless and Lysol disinfected of 99.9% germs. All the garish color of the *Family Double Dare* set seems to fade as Marc introduces the challenge, and the stage is now bathed in a warm golden light. Marc sets the timer for thirty seconds and singsongs the cue: "Audience, cheer them on! On your mark . . . get set . . . goooo!"

Eggbert runs across the stage into the arms of Mr. HYPNO who lifts him in a big spinning hug. Eggbert then runs back across the stage, turns around, and does it again. Each time Mr. HYPNO lifts Eggbert into the air, they pause for a moment and point at the Gladwell family, incriminating them, before beaming again with happiness as Eggbert alights to the stage. It is a "Hug & Point" relay. Every time team HYPNO points at the Gladwell family, the gesture is accompanied by the sound effect of a large dog barking ferociously.

Their success at the relay wins them five thousand dollars. The splashy colors return to the *Family Double Dare* set. "This is the type of physical activity that will bring value to your life," Mr. HYPNO tells Eggbert, grasping his shoulders and looking him straight in the eyes. "It is physical labor to love someone. It is psychic labor to know your parents have wronged you."

Mr. HYPNO helps Marc challenge Eggbert's family to answer other questions they don't have answers for: Mrs. Gladwell, why did you settle for Mr. Gladwell? Mr. Gladwell, how do you feel about yourself after spending two hundred dollars for a happy ending at the massage parlor on Ketchikan Road? Neurotypical

Gladwell son, are you aware that your father is spending your college fund on two-hundred-dollar handjobs from an undocumented Korean masseuse named Chung-Cha Lee? Neurotypical Gladwell son, why do you tell your friends at school that Eggbert was adopted? Mrs. Gladwell, can you guess how many times Chung-Cha Lee has given your husband a handjob? Mr. and Mrs. Gladwell, is there any shame in admitting you weren't mentally prepared for a child with special needs? Gladwell family, when was the last time you really felt like a family?

Mr. HYPNO makes sure that Eggbert gets to watch his family complete many more exciting Physical Challenges. He watches his family eat hundred-dollar bills out of each other's mouths. He watches his family pick up novelty oversized telephones to try and communicate with dead relatives, only to hear people screaming in torment on the other end of the line. He watches his family strip naked and don suits made of rotted meat to try and sell used Isuzus to audience members, though no one is buying. Eggbert still believes this is all just a game, laughing and clapping as he watches his family rapidly age and crash into their fated futures: his father alone and alcoholic, covered in red sores, his mother living with her extended family in Fredericksburg, addicted to opiates after a back injury, his brother a philanderer who destroys those he loves for sport. Each of the Physical Challenges takes several years to complete.

The audience is going apeshit.

Eggbert whispers something to Mr. HYPNO.

"Excuse me, Marc," says Mr. HYPNO. "We are done with the game. Eggbert wants to run the final obstacle course."

"Yes, of course!" says Marc. The Gladwell family, utterly broken, is ushered backstage.

"Eggbert deserves all of the prizes," says Mr. HYPNO, "and if anyone here thinks that's unfair, they should ponder the meaning of fairness."

"I understand," says Marc.

"Eggbert deserves the British Knights shoes and the Nickelodeon fun package. He deserves the trip to Coconut Bay in the Bahamas and he deserves the Sony camcorder. He deserves the Huffy bike, the Conair hair dryer, the state-of-the-art karaoke machine, and the deluxe sports set with the hockey gear. He's going to play hockey."

"I understand," says Marc.

"He is going to play hockey and he's going to be a champion, and when he looks back across the years, upon the wife he's loved and the children he's sired and the trophies he's won and the millions of fans he's inspired, he's going to remember the hockey sticks that he won here today, courtesy of Spalding sporting goods."

"It's true," says Marc.

American Daydream

"But first he's going to run the obstacle course, pulling the flag out of the giant boogery nose, squeezing his gangly body through the paint rollers, sliding down the slide into the chocolate pudding, working his way across the monkey bars over the vat of whipped cream, diving into the giant gumball machine and dispensing himself. His effort will be rewarded with fifty thousand dollars. No, make it a hundred thousand. And, Marc, we're going to give him all the time he needs. I see you ready to set the timer for sixty seconds. Set the timer for sixty years. Six hundred years. Six thousand miles. He can change his name if he likes. He's going to win the Stanley Cup. Nothing can stop him. Nobody. He's going to be wearing British Knights sneakers in the fucking Bahamas, Marc! And he's going to capture every triumphant moment he has there on his brand-new Sony camcorder! He's going to start off every day singing 'We Are the Champions' with his state-of-the-art karaoke machine! Do you understand me?"

Marc nods. Mr. HYPNO turns toward the audience. He faces America. His eyes have slit pupils, like a snake. He paints a broad smile on his face and grabs Eggbert's hand, raising his arm victoriously into the air. "Audience," he says, "cheer him on."

— Tagert Ellis

3.

The *Are You Smarter than a 5th Grader?* audience wasn't watching. The audience never watched the actual show anymore. They only watched the freckled little ten-year-old named Shiny. Some held signs. Some brought their old and their sick and their prayers. Shiny sat serenely at his desk, levitating a few inches above his seat, emitting the glittery powder blue aura he wouldn't (no matter how many times Fox Jefferson begged him) stop radiating.

Fox quipped. Fox capered. The neon red "CHEER NOW" signs flashed their one command. But the audience wasn't watching. Not even the kids on stage were watching. They were supposed to laugh at Fox's jokes, to show he was the "cool teacher." Ever since Shiny had joined the "class" and the kids had all gotten that dumb enraptured look on their faces like they'd just seen a baby panda cuddling a kitten, Fox's antics had become less and less effective, more and more desperate. At least no one seemed to notice.

Just a few weeks ago the kids on the show used to act like kids. When Fox puffed his cheeks and contorted his salt-and-pepper eyebrows into his "comedian face," everyone would laugh. When the interns came around with juice boxes, the kids wanted juice boxes. Shiny, too, would take a juice box, turning it over in his pink hands, studying its corners, its bright cartoon apples and grapes. Then Shiny would blink twice, and the juice box would warp and twist impossibly before contracting to an infinitesimal point and vanishing altogether. *Ahhh,* Shiny would say, looking around for more juice boxes. Now the kids line up to kneel before Shiny and offer him their juice boxes.

Tonight's contestant was Brad Something, who at first glance seemed like the kind of guy who'd go on TV wearing a thousand-dollar suit in need of tailoring. Fox checked the length of Brad's coat sleeves to see if they were too long, and smirked. Some things, at least, went on as always. "All right, Brad, time to choose," Fox said, like a game show host who still believed in free will. "Who would you like to pick as your classmate? This is a big decision, Brad, because the student you choose will be able to help you answer one question . . ."

Fox willed the other kids to wiggle and wave, to yell *me me me!* Instead they watched Shiny bluely radiate, and from time to time wept tears of unalloyed joy. Brad chose, of course, Shiny, who floated to the podium, calm as a precious stone.

The lights danced over the audience; the canned orchestra swelled, and Fox strutted to center stage. Shiny or no Shiny, this was the part Fox loved most, the moment just before it really started, when anything could happen. "Here we go, Brad! Your first question—"

Cincinnati, Fox heard in his mind, as they all heard in their minds.

"Cincinnati," said Brad. His winnings flashed on the screen, $1,000.

Quarks. Geodes. The War of 1812. Shiny glowed brighter, his golden curls blown by inexplicable winds. Brad's score went up and up.

This was bad TV, Fox knew. Bad TV had been made flesh, and bad TV was a bucktoothed little doofus with freckles, whose parents (did he have parents?) dressed him in sweater vests, and who could, admittedly, levitate. "Now Brad, let me ask you something." Fox paused dramatically, scrutinizing the contestant, raising one eyebrow and shaking his head, employing every trick he knew to heighten the theatrical suspense. "Why is it—"

"Because we *experience* time as a line, Mr. Jefferson," Brad said in a young boy's soprano, "the same way a moth *experiences* a lightbulb as the moon. But *we* know the lightbulb is not the moon. Do you see, Mr. Jefferson?"

Midway down Row 10, a guy who had come in on crutches was dancing atop his seat. An old lady's dead cat sprang from its shoebox coffin and purringly rubbed against her legs.

Rhizomes. Greenland. Brad's total ticked up to its sixth figure.

They had reached the Final Question. "All right, Brad, this is it! You can walk away now with five hundred *thousand* dollars," Fox leaned forward, gripping his podium, "or you can risk it all!"

Shiny was now hovering three yards above the stage, arms open in a gesture of bountiful peace. His aura was almost blinding. Brad's ill-fitting suit was bursting with rays of holy light. The contestant closed his eyes and opened his mouth to give praise, unleashing a sound like all the glass on earth singing in chorus.

Deep in his body, in some layer of himself buried beneath the Hollywood, Fox heard—*felt*—Shiny's call, as they all felt Shiny's call: *Follow me, friends. There is nothing to fear. You've all won.* One by one, classmates and Brad and live studio audience alike began to float, to hum and glow until their bodies were things of pure light. A white flash, the glassy song crescendoing to a deafening tsunami of celestial gongs, then nothing. When the blind spots began to shrink and the world's shapes resolved themselves, Fox raised his downcast eyes to scan the studio. But he already knew that he was alone. The seats held only clothes emptied of bodies. Where Shiny had been, a powder blue crystalline egg thrummed.

Fox ran backstage, through the empty dressing rooms, out to the empty hall, out to the empty lot, calling out at first, then screaming, then cackling, then silence. He sat in the middle of the street, looked up and down the road to each horizon, and laid his head down on the warm asphalt.

The sun was beginning to dip below the tree line when Fox woke up, and still no people, only abandoned cars and shops. The audience, the classmates, the viewers at home—everyone must be somewhere else now, some*thing* else. Fox grunted to his feet, cracked his stiff back, and ambled toward the studio. He'd never be in a hurry again.

Inside, Shiny's crystal egg had swollen to three times its original size and now gave off a thin, power station whine. The "CHEER NOW" signs were still lit up, and they filled the studio with an incubator's warm, dim redness. Fox wrapped the egg in Brad's empty suit for warmth, tucking the bundle safe beneath his podium. He didn't know what else to do, and it's what the folks at home would have wanted.

— J. G. McClure

4.

Flipping through the channels in your endless pursuit of entertainment, you come across *The Amazing Race*.

The sun is setting over a long, rural stretch of highway. "We're low on gas," says the woman in the driver seat, a frazzled-looking blonde who might be a model or dancer of some sort. You can tell by the hair extensions and breast implants that she's obsessed with her appearance. "How much money do we have left?"

"I gave everything we had to a homeless person back at the last stop," says her partner, a very thin man with translucent skin and a Beatles mop-top haircut, outfitted in a powder blue tuxedo complete with ruffled shirt and bowtie. "It seemed like the right thing to do."

"Are you kidding me?"

"I'm sure someone will pay for our gas once we get to the next station."

"Who's going to ask for spare change? You? You don't speak Bulgarian, do you?"

"I'm fluent in human."

"Keep telling yourself that," she says. They're not a couple. That's obvious. You wonder how they ended up on the same team. Coworkers, maybe?

"I'm sensing you're distraught," says her diaphanous partner, pressing his index fingers against his temples. "If you'd like, I could massage your anahata chakra."

"I don't think that's legal in this country," she says jokingly. He doesn't seem to get it.

"In that case, would you like me to tune your chi?"

"It's working just fine, thanks."

"Perhaps I could—

"Don't you know how to do anything useful?"

He looks surprised by the question. "Sure, I can slow my heartrate down to six beats per minute."

She looks at him and rolls her eyes. The car swerves in the same direction she turns her head. Only for a second. Two seconds longer and they would have been in a wreck. Leaning forward and resting on the steering wheel, she yawns, then blinks her drooping eyes several times in quick succession. "Can you take the wheel for a while? I'm getting sleepy."

"I only know how to drive the psyche. But don't worry, I have a hunch we'll be there soon."

She lets out a frustrated sigh. "Could you at least look at the map and see if we're going the right way?"

"Something tells me we are. I can feel it."

"Seriously, I need some help here!"

"I am helping, in my own way. I'm remaining calm."

"Stop being so calm all the time! It's freaking me out!"

"Everything's going to be all right. You just need to relax. Take a deep breath."

"Don't tell me how to breathe!" She takes short, quick breaths just to spite him, hyperventilating herself.

As a familiar band starts to play and the camera shot pans out, you realize this is not an episode of *The Amazing Race*. It is a parody of *The Amazing Race* on *Saturday Night Live*. You turn off the television and flip open your laptop, deciding you'd rather watch a rerun of the real version of *The Amazing Race* on YouTube. And then you remember that none of this is real (partly because the narrator just reminded you). This is merely a fictional story, most of which is a parody of *Saturday Night Live* doing a parody of *The Amazing Race*. You wonder what else isn't real. Only for a minute. Two minutes longer and you would have vanished entirely.

— J. Martin Strangeweather

5.

It had begun in the nineties as an anti-pageant pageant, but no one over the age of eight really believed it was countercultural anymore. The founders would meet in a Geary Boulevard bookshop after closing and take turns parading across the cinderblock stage set up in front of the classics section, flipping their bad haircuts, licking their pocket protectors seductively while quoting Heidegger or Nagarjuna or some other brainy dead guy, reciting pi to a hundred and fifty digits, hooting for one another and huffing on inhalers that, according to some fans, were loaded with nitrous oxide cartridges. Back then, the winner was crowned with a wreath of melted action figures, and there was no prize money involved. A certain Mr. Gary Shepherd, software mogul, recently purchased the original wreath for 1.2 million dollars at a well-publicized auction.

The whole thing would have run its course in the cluttered ten feet of runway between Austen and Zola if Jeb Fisher, the infamous producer of such classic competitions as *Pastry Smackdown* and *Bridal Force*, hadn't been in the area scouting for talent at the *Real Reality* competition, where it was rumored a bright young go-getter had put together a pitch called *The Big*

Freeze in which newlyweds cohabitated for as long as they could in a cold storage facility. When it turned out the go-getter was just looking for a free place to live, a disappointed Fisher took to the town, and midnight found him stumbling out of The Sleazy Producer a block north of the bookshop after one too many whisky sours, rattling the bookshop's locked doors, demanding "a cheap copy of the Kama Sutra or anything by de Sade" just as Regina Portman, a pasty-faced beaut in a pink nylon windbreaker and matching fannypack, was reciting the periodic table and performing an "alchemical" interpretive dance routine. Spying her through the storefront window as she became the embodiment of beryllium, he fell in love on the spot. Unable to distinguish the woman from the competition, he felt compelled to produce it. Claim it. Make it his in a legally binding manner.

Only twice had a female contestant made it to the final three. No woman had ever won. Margo Wicker was going to be the first. Margo had wanted to be a contestant on *America's Next Top Nerd* ever since she was a know-it-all three-year-old with glittery gold glasses strapped to her head like goggles so she wouldn't lose them. Each year, she put the winner's official poster—$49.99 for the limited-edition signed version (plus shipping and handling)— on the ceiling above her bed. Her dreams were a pageant of thick glasses and polyhedral dice, tinfoil cosplay and braces muddy from chocolate, intellect outshining ever-changing constellations of zit cream. By all rights, it should have been her. She was a three-time science fair winner, a self-published novelist, a falconer, had mossy teeth and a perceptible mustache since birth, and was so hopeless with small talk she tended to wince and rub her eyes whenever anyone mentioned the subject of weather. Her younger sister Penelope, on the other hand, was dewy-skinned and downy-haired, with big wet eyes and giraffe legs and a knack for superficial conversation, making her a favorite at school. Her ineptitude at all things nerdly was so painfully conspicuous that Margo had to wear earplugs just to ride in the same car with her on family outings. She thought zombies, werewolves, and vampires were basically the same thing, had never watched a documentary of any sort, and didn't even know how to use a protractor. Margo would not, could not stand the silly things her sister said. Margo would not, could not stand the vapid magazines her sister read. Margo didn't like her sister's favorite hangout place, the mall. Margo didn't like her sister much at all. Nevertheless, when she and Margo were eighteen and twenty-one respectively, Margo agreed to let her younger sister accompany her to a hard-won audition for the show at NBC Studios in 30 Rockefeller Plaza.

Twenty minutes before her fate would be decided, Margo was slouched in the waiting room on a metal folding chair alongside nineteen other frizzy-haired, overeducated young people with pronounced body odor and curdled saliva in the corners of their mouths, cooing to her falcon, Galadriel. Penelope was dancing in the hallway to a K-pop mix on her iPod. Her failure at nerdhood had left her with few other alternatives but to study ballet as a child, and she still moved with the delicate precision of a blooming orchid. She rose to her toes en pointe and posed arabesque against a large portrait of Jeb Fisher framed ornately in gold. She wasn't stupid, despite whatever Margo said. Her mind was just lighter and more open than her sister's, devoid of those hard little knots of obsessive puzzle-solving, adrift in gauzy half-ideas. She would rather not know the names of birds, because then she could see their colors better. When it came to certain things, she knew how to do them almost instinctively, like riding a horse, and ballroom dancing. Whenever she caught the wafting scent of breakfast cooking in some random house on her walk to school, she liked to stop and linger in the gathering daylight, learning every note of the fragrance. She was often late to class.

From his desk in the glass office at the end of the hall, the payroll clerk was translating the esoteric language of her graceful movements. The payroll clerk had never seen her before, but he instantly recognized her. He had known her in many different incarnations spanning many past lifetimes. Known her, and cared for her. Loved her. Of this he was sure. She had been his mother, his sister, his daughter, and in some lives, his lover. Romantics refer to this as *love at first sight*. He sidled up and tapped her on the back of her shoulder. "Excuse me," he said. "But did you know that the word *nerd* first appeared in Doctor Seuss's *If I Ran the Zoo*? Apparently it doesn't mean what we think it does."

She twirled around to face him with her arms above her head shaping the foliage of an imaginary tree. "Did you know Fruit Loops are all the same flavor?" She didn't know this herself, but still, it came out of her mouth.

"Did you know Einstein turned down the presidency of Israel in 1952?"

"Did you know ravens are better than parrots at mimicking human speech?"

They faced each other. Seconds ticked by, feeling like centuries. Penelope let her arms bloom out and fall to her sides. The payroll clerk bowed like he really meant it. He was a young man in his early twenties with a puffy blond afro and a wheeze-whistle nose. He wore a powder blue tuxedo complemented with a ruffled shirt and bowtie, which would have seemed oddly out of place on anyone else, but on him it seemed perfectly appropriate. The tux's breast pocket held a pink handkerchief that lolled out like a tongue as he bowed. "Trancelot Fletcher, humble payroll clerk, lover of crossword puzzles, three-time Ferris-wheel-accident-survivor."

Penelope could not decide whether to ask him about his name or the Ferris wheel accidents. Inside the waiting room, a Harry Potter wannabe was tinkering with a pocket chemistry kit, charming iridescent smoke from a miniature Erlenmeyer flask.

Margo was trying to coax Galadriel off the receptionist's head. "What kind of a name is Trancelot?"

He smiled. His teeth were chalky with toothpaste residue. "When I was born, my mother thought my eyes were hypnotic. Do *you* think so?"

"I guess so." People thought she couldn't think, but she could, it was just hard for her to put what she was thinking into words, not like Margo who would stand under the sycamore in the yard and scream, "Waldeinsamkeit!" as if her soul was sneezing.

"Mother told me this was an auspicious day," said Trancelot. "She has a sense for these things." He breathed on his palm and sniffed it, checking the status of his breath, then straightened his bowtie and made sure his ruffled shirt was uniformly tucked in. "I'm just going to come right out and say it," he said, playfully poking the tip of her nose, "I think you're cooler than Spock singing 'The Ballad of Bilbo Baggins.'" She understood, even though she didn't grasp the literal meaning.

"But you've barely just met me," she said.

Trancelot grinned. "Time is relative."

"I don't know what that means," she said, looking down and fidgeting with a strand of her hair. "I'm not smart. Not in the right way, anyway."

Trancelot took Penelope by the hand and led her into his office. "You need to stop telling yourself things like that," gesturing for her to take a seat. "It's nonsense. There is no right way.

Everyone's smart in their *own* way, and dumb in their own way, too. I'll prove it. Have you ever heard of the power of suggestion?"

"Maybe."

"Well, I have the *superpower* of suggestion. What if I told you that you're going to win this competition?"

"No, I'm just waiting for my sister."

"Listen to me, and please listen closely. You're very bright, very sanctimonious, and you can type one hundred and eighty words per minute."

"What's sanctimo—

"You can solve a Rubik's Cube in less than ten seconds, you've been playing *Dungeons & Dragons* since you were five, and you can see twenty-three moves ahead in chess."

"I've never even played checkers."

"You've memorized the lineage of all the Egyptian, Chinese, and European royal families," continued Trancelot, speaking directly to the all-hearing ear of her subconscious, summoning forth ghostly legions of knowledge she had passively absorbed throughout her life but never harnessed into meaningful experience, unlocking genetic insights from countless other lifetimes as well. "You're trying to breed a pet unicorn, you built your first Tesla coil at the age of twelve, and you can juggle six calculators at once."

"Whatever you're doing, it's working," said Penelope. "I think I'm starting to remember memories that aren't mine." She closed her eyes and concentrated. "In one of them I'm a geologist whose favorite pastime is reading about our planet's dwindling supply of sand. In another I'm a chef who refuses to eat anything spelled with the letter E, and in another my favorite color is X-ray, except I'm so nerdy I call it Roentgen ray." She opened her eyes, looking astonished. "But I've never even heard of a Roentgen ray."

"If you were to trace your lineage back for ten generations, you would discover over a thousand ancestors in your family tree, and if you were to trace your lineage back for twenty generations, you would discover millions! Myriad nerds lie dormant within your bloodline! Awaken, oh dweebs!" He took a moment to catch his breath, wheezing terribly. "You're getting nerdier by the second. Is that a pimple I see sprouting on your chin?"

Her hand flew to a tingling sensation on her face. Under her fingers swelled something alien to her experience, pus-filled and painful, like a throbbing little volcano.

"The process of retrocognitive reawakening can be somewhat unsettling," he said. "How are you feeling?"

She felt like herself, but more so. "Is this fair?" she said. "I mean, to the other contestants?"

"Was it fair when you were burned at the stake for witchcraft?" said Trancelot. "Eternity has its own way of balancing everything out."

"But what about my sister?"

"Her turn will come again. It's your turn now."

She looked into his eyes, so big and blue, and she felt herself rising toward them.

The way the gossip magazines told it, Penelope burst in during Margo's audition, corrected her as to the boiling point of mercury, and plucked the glasses right off her face, but no one other than the few people in the room that day will ever really know for sure. What everyone and their grandma does know is how the casting directors went gaga over Penelope, and how Margo was seen weeping at arcades for almost a year before she married the associate producer of the rip-off *Nerd Alert*, and how now she broods in her New Jersey mansion reading murder mystery novels all day, but only those written by female authors. Fans of *America's Next Top Nerd* remember Penelope for the savage brilliance with which she took down her competitors by sabotaging their inhalers and slipping them spurious facts about the "true" identity of historical personages such as Homer and Shakespeare and Banksy, the hour-long speech she gave in Esperanto when she won her tenth wreath. As the years went by, one could not help but notice the hair on her limited-edition signed portraits go from downy to stringy, and the acne scars amassing to blot out her pretty face, her body growing lumpy under those thick wool sweaters she always wore.

The night of her first major victory (i.e., winning season 11, outnerding a total of ninety-nine other Dilberts and Poindexters, including her sister, over the course of ten mind-numbing episodes), she and Trancelot eschewed the party given in her honor. Instead she put on oversized sunglasses and a furry cap with earflaps, and they went bowling.

"My darling Sir Trancelot," she said, hefting the ball and lining it up to roll over the second arrow, calculating the rate of curvature, "am I truly a nerd?"

"You are *the* nerd," he wheezed. "The nerd's nerd. You are the nerdiest nerd ever to wheeze for dear breath. Your nerditude knows no bounds. According to mother, you were Laura Bassi, the first woman to hold a teaching position at the University of Bologna. You've also been the seventh Duchess of Bedford, Anna Russell, credited with establishing the British afternoon tea ceremony. In ancient times you were a Spartan lyric poetess named Clitagora, and in prehistoric times you were Kathara, the High Priestess of Atlantis, among many other nerdly and noble incarnations." He bowed to her, as he had when they first met. "At your service, now and forever, your nerdness."

She grinned, turned around, and threw the ball with perfect aim, but it slowed to a crawl halfway down the lane, taking a full fifteen seconds to reach the pin deck, barely tapping the foremost pin. She lacked the strength to throw a twelve-pound bowling ball effectively, having grown much weaker since her intellectual reawakening. She sat down. Trancelot rubbed her shoulders, and she became sleepy. "I once had a dream that everyone was smarter than me, and they would tease me, and bully me."

"And?"

"It was strange, the dream, like experiencing someone else's memories."

These days, Penelope is retired and doesn't remember much about her rise to dweeby stardom, considering herself more of an eccentric recluse now than anything else. She likes to collect antique pocket watches and dissect them, artfully spangling the walls, cabinets, countertops, and other surfaces of her apartment with clockwork innards. Her apartment is a rococo Eden in the glass tip of a rocket-shaped tower in lower Manhattan, where she lives with her husband, a humble payroll clerk. Trancelot stays out late on Long Island most nights helping his debilitated mother, whom he claims is the reincarnation of Helena Blavatsky. Penelope doesn't mind the solitude. Trancelot gives her moonrock jewelry on their anniversaries, and edits her occasional nerd lifestyle book. Sometimes she calls her sister, usually on her birthday. Sometimes her sister answers. Their conversations consist mostly of remorseful sighs between long intervals of uncomfortable silence. Penelope sees a therapist once a week to work through her imposter syndrome.

In the apartment downstairs, where the Fletchers' floor is someone else's ceiling, a plump girl with braces and enormous

American Daydream

ears has the limited-edition signed poster of Penelope looking down at her from above her bed. Her twin sister, a thinner, prettier version of herself wearing too much lipstick, spends her time gazing out the bedroom window at clouds and skyscrapers, thinking about boys.

— Martina Hutchins

6.

Hey there, naked man. I see you coming toward me across the sand dunes, your wavy silhouette sizzling in the heat like the obligatory desert mirage. I hope the cameraman's got a good angle on you. I also hope you're the forgiving kind, because I have a confession to make. Let's just say I "embellished the facts" on my audition tape. When I said I learned to skeet shoot before kindergarten? Nope. Brown belt in Brazilian Jiu-jitsu? Not really. And those survivalist stories are strictly imaginary; I couldn't start a fire with a blowtorch and a can of gasoline, nor have I ever cooked and eaten anything scraped off the side of the road. On the contrary, I grew up in a McMansion in Irvine with two older sisters, an inground pool, a Viking fridge the size of a walk-in closet, and a Pekinese dog named Bushels. When I met the producers in person I could tell they were having trouble squaring my mousey, blink-and-you'll-miss-her presence with my bogus résumé. I am so unexceptional in fact, that when I told the casting director the only true thing about me—that I'm a survivor of sexual assault—he yawned.

These days, he must have thought, *everyone's a victim of something*.

American Daydream

I'm used to being trivialized—to being immaterial to the plot line. I wear my invisibility like a magic cloak or ring; that is, I wear it to my advantage. It turns out my trumped-up résumé was too juicy to pass up, because here I am, at long last, in Lençóis Maranhenses National Park, Brazil, ready as I'll ever be to do battle with sand, heat, dehydration, and you.

There are three basic kinds of male contestants on *Naked and Afraid*: The Survivalist, The Marine, and The Motivational Speaker. As you come closer, making a token effort to cover your private parts with the canvas bag you're carrying—still portraying yourself as a gentleman—I feel you out, so to speak. Toned but not buff, with a hieroglyphic eye tattooed over your heart and a palpable aura of confidence and joviality, you're a collage of all three types of contestants. Your face reminds me of my cousin Tad—sort of piscine with wide, powder blue eyes and an easygoing smile that offsets your rather plain looks. To be honest, I'm disappointed with how average you are. I'm afraid we'll both be so boring we'll cancel each other out, which is bad for prime-time ratings—and especially bad for my *Vice* essay, which is why I'm really here.

The show draws viewers by pairing contestants who have opposite personalities, maximizing the prospect for drama. The producers think I'm a backwoods feminist, so naturally I expected them to set me up with a rapey Republican gun nut. But somebody in central casting must have missed the memo—you seem about as dangerous as a head of lettuce. What's the lede, I wonder, quickly reconsidering my possible story arcs. I can already sense "Iraq War Veteran Goes Ballistic in Desert Paradise" is not going to happen. Neither is "Recovering Scientologist Rediscovers Xenu" or "Shocking Finale: Contestant Confesses to Triple Homicide!" You're just too damned ordinary for any of these headlines. And romance, of course, is out of the question. Sex never happens on the show, contestants being too hungry and dirty for it. But I will figure you out, in a narratively satisfying way. I've got three weeks to mold you into a compelling artifact of the twenty-first century. You're in good hands. It's what I get paid to do.

You're trying hard not to let your eyes wander south of my chin. That's okay, there's plenty of time for that. For now you keep your wide-eyed gaze trained on mine, and you mumble, "Let's get this over with," and I mumble back, "It is what it is," like every other contestant on this show. We shake hands. It occurs to me this is the happiest and cleanest we'll be for the next twenty-one days. Like the viewers watching at home, my hope is that hunger, thirst, and mosquitoes will provoke us into becoming more interesting.

You tell me your name is Frank Mesmermann, but sometimes you go by Franky Mesmerelli or Francisco Mesmerino, and you are the great-great-great grandson of Franz Mesmer, the German father of animal magnetism. "German," you say, as if there are also Swiss fathers, Korean fathers, Senegalese and Croatian fathers, each with his own style of metaphysical chicanery. I take note of this nontrivial piece of information and store it away for later use. You've just become more interesting, with your absurd aliases and dubious heritage and the possibility you might be a neo-Nazi. I tell you my name, and nothing else. You ask what's in my messenger bag, and I show you my match kit. "Good one," you say. "What about you?" I ask. You show me a thick roll of duct tape—durable and water-resistant and perfect for tying up wrists and ankles. Sorry not sorry, that's just how I tend to see things nowadays, and who can blame me? Maybe the arc of my *Vice* article is how you will kill me, and how I will die. I wonder if you'll do it slow or make it quick.

They say serial killers always seem very normal. I don't know if they really say that, but it is kind of a trope. You seem very normal, almost too normal. You do, however, have a nice ass. Just saying, if I have to look at it every day for the next three weeks. Your ass gives me reassurance. No way would a man who looks like he does Bulgarian Squats and Star Jump Burpees kill people to get his kicks. I follow you across the desert, looking at your ass, while the cameraman follows me, possibly looking at mine. Probably not. I'm sure he's seen lots of asses in his day. Maybe he doesn't even see asses anymore, only the interplay between light and shadow.

The sand is soft and deep. It sucks our feet down. We make slow progress.

We stop under a lone palm tree near a turquoise lagoon about the size of my pool back home. You glance at the cameraman, and in turn the cameraman glances at me. I try not to imagine that the two of you are in cahoots, cooking up a treacherous plan using some sort of frat-boy telepathy. I'm of the opinion that everyone is psychic to a certain extent, empathy presumably being the most common psychic ability. I have the power to read anyone's mind except my own, or so I've been told by one of my exes.

Curiously enough, trying not to imagine that the two of you are in cahoots involves imagining the two of you in cahoots. Cynics say everyone is guilty until proven innocent. I go one step further and say everyone is guilty until proven guiltier.

You sit down and pat the sand next to you, and I join you as you outline your strategy. There's sand in my crack. It feels extremely unpleasant. "We'll build a shelter here using some of these palm fronds," you say. "We need to shield ourselves from the sun. Thirst won't be a problem; the lagoon water is drinkable, but we'll have to boil it. Do you hunt? I do. I'm a good hunter, so no worries there." You point at things with two fingers and squint as you talk, like Clint Eastwood, or a no-nonsense drill sergeant from the movies, only much friendlier.

For me, "roughing it" means a hotel with no room service, so in spite of myself, I admire the way you take charge. Your pectorals flex as you gesticulate, I can't help but notice. I also notice you're careful to soften your tone as you address me, asking if I have anything to add to the plan, to which I respond, "Not really." Your Ivy League haircut says corporate and your straight white teeth say meticulous. I'm going to guess you sit behind a desk and make uncannily prescient ad-hoc decisions. It's obvious you know how to grill a decent steak. Feeling more comfortable around you, I ask what the duct tape is for.

"Good question," you say. "I suppose now is as good a time as any."

You reach into your bag and bring out the roll. "Please understand, it's nothing personal." You tear off several feet of tape, folding the strip in half and adhering the halves together to reinforce them, then folding the strip in other, more curious ways. You do the same with another stretch of tape, making terrible ripping sounds as you create what I can only imagine are my restraints. When you have three reinforced lengths of duct tape resting in your lap—two to bind my arms and legs and one to put over my mouth—you nod to the cameraman and ask me to turn away from you. I consider fleeing. I consider fighting. But the line in the sand hasn't been crossed yet. There's still a good chance you're not a homicidal rapist.

"Sorry," you say as you reach around my torso with the tape. You tell me this is for my own good, and that I'm right to be wary of regular guys, they're the most dangerous. How are you inside my head, I wonder. But mostly I'm wondering how they will find me—in bloody chunks, or maybe lying at the bottom of the lagoon with a purple neck. I feel sorry for friends and family who might see the coroner's photos. I wonder if my editor at *Vice* will feel remorse. Already a part of me feels responsible for the cancellation of *Naked and Afraid*, which has been running for a full ten seasons.

"The target demographic for this show believes sociopathic behavior is typical," your voice echoes in my head, or maybe the heat is getting to me and I'm starting to hear things. You hold the band of duct tape in front of my chest and lay it across my breasts. You bring the ends around and hold them together against my back. "Too tight?" you ask.

"I don't know," I say, confused. You tie the ends together.

"I'm guessing this is your first time wearing a duct-tape bra," you say. "It isn't Victoria's Secret, but it'll do." You hand me another of your duct-tape improvisations and invite me to try it on. It's a pair of undies, sort of. I can see you've also taped together a pair of underwear for yourself. The funny thing is, I'm totally fine with being nude. That's half the reason I'm here.

"It's not you, it's me," you say, seeming to be in my head again, or is my imagination getting the better of me? "I hope you don't mind." I sort of do. Who are you to deprive the viewers of what they want?

American Daydream

Fastening my silvery makeshift bikini bottom, I realize your storyline, the tale of the quintessential American male, is refusing my desire to scandalize you. I'm panicking again, but this time it's a privileged sort of panic, the bougie, writerly panic I feel when I spot a typo after hitting "send." I rethink my possible arcs. "Eagle Scout Strips Down and Mans Up." Boring. "Demure Dreamboat Docks in Desert Oasis." Bleh! Nothing you do on this show will ever be as compelling as "Starving Contestant Resorts to Eating the Camera Crew" or even just "Contestant Makes Inappropriate Sexual Advances." You defy the narrative of our angry, man-hating generation. Part of me almost wants to see if I can trip you up. But it wouldn't be right. Yours is a story the world must know, the non-toxic, gluten-free, all-natural side of masculinity, the safe side, the thrillingly average side.

The sun, just moments before a blinding eye of unyielding misery, is now a dusky beacon of possibilities. There's a cool breeze coming in from the coast. Sunlight bathes the landscape in gold, glinting off the surface of the lagoon and the contours of our bodies, filling our sandy footprints with sparkling flecks.

"We'll be fine," you say. "Just you wait and see, the time will go by like *that*," and you snap your fingers. Why didn't I see it before? The patience and generosity etched into the lines of your face, so handsome in its own humble way, so adept at becoming whatever I want. Letting my imagination wander, I see the heat and pressure of our predicament fusing us into the couple we could be, the couple we were meant to be, the two of us embracing during the season finale like lovers in a storybook.

I wonder if you feel the same way about me, imagining you do.

54

— L. Joyce Morel

7.

"Hey, good to see you all," says Pat Sajak, addressing the contestants on *Wheel of Fortune*. "Let's get started, shall we? This toss-up puzzle is worth one thousand dollars, and the category is *tautology*." Letters begin lighting up on the board, one after the other. First an *O*, then a *T*, another *O*, an *I*, a *W*, and the contestant behind the red podium rings in.

"Winners don't lose," he answers.

"They sure don't," says Pat, and the studio audience cheers. "Milton Mulroney," says Pat, speaking to the contestant behind the red podium, "from Des Moines, Iowa."

"That's right, Pat."

Pat looks without pretense at the cards in his hand. "It says here you love your job."

"Sure do, Pat. I'm a certified—

"Nobody cares!" says the contestant standing behind the yellow podium with Braino scrawled on his nametag. He growls the words, as if possessed by a demon. "Spin the wheel already!" He's wearing thick black square glasses, the bridge of which is padded with tape. The lenses are so scratched you can't see his eyes. His clothes are torn, and not in the fashionable way. You can't help but notice that his powder blue tuxedo is stained with what appears to be blood.

"Uh, you heard the man," says Pat. "Spin that wheel and let's see what happens. The category for the first round is *blasphemous phrase*." He gives Vanna White a confused look. She shrugs her shoulders. "Is that right?" he says to someone offstage.

The contestant behind the red podium leans over and gives the wheel a spin. His flipper lands on a $600 wedge of the wheel. "I'll have a *D* please."

"There are two *D*'s." Two of the white rectangles on the board light up in blue, prompting Vanna to come and touch them, revealing the letter. She used to have an actual function when the board was composed of trilons that had to be manually turned. You force yourself to ignore her obsolescence, otherwise you'll spend the rest of the show feeling sorry for her.

"I'd like to solve the puzzle, Pat."

"Let's hear it."

"*Bleep! Bleep! Bleep!*"

"Unfortunately that's incorrect," says Pat. "Braino, your turn."

"I'd like to buy a vowel," snarls Braino.

"Sorry, Braino," says Pat. His smile looks strained. "You haven't won any money yet."

"I'd like to borrow some from Milton."

American Daydream

Pat chuckles nervously. "Have you ever watched an episode of this game before?" He's turning red, getting flustered. "Go ahead and take a chance at the wheel."

"Chance?" growls Braino. "What is chance? Order and disorder are illusions of mortal perspective. All is madness." He readjusts his glasses, going from crooked to crookeder. "Through my belief-lenses, the madness appears ordered in some ways and disordered in others. Through your belief-lenses, the madness could very well appear oppositely ordered and disordered." Readjusting his glasses, he accidentally knocks them off and then bangs his head against the podium rail as he bends over to pick them up. He puts them on upside down, wisps of his comb-over jutting wildly. "Luck's for the luckless. Sometimes you just have to sway the odds, put weights on the fates, you know, rig the game." He winks at Pat indiscreetly.

The game show host looks unnerved.

Braino reaches over and slowly turns the wheel until his flipper is pointing to the $2500 wedge.

"You can't do that, Braino!" says Pat.

"I'd like to solve the puzzle, Pat!" He clears his throat. "I know all about what happened at that party in the summer of '86."

Pat looks caught red-handed. Vanna's mouth is agape.

— Mr. Fucko

8.

"Welcome to *Family Feud* everybody. I'm your main man, Steve Harvey, and we've got another great episode for y'all today. From Broken Arrow, Oklahoma, it's the White family!" Everything about Steve Harvey is oversized: his shiny blue suit, his caterpillar mustache, his blinding white teeth, which barely seem to fit in his mouth, and his ego. "And all the way from Jackson, Mississippi, it's the Black family!"

The audience responds with obligatory excitement.

"It's time to start the feud," says Steve. "Get yourselves on up here!" The show's energetic theme music plays and the audience claps to the rhythm.

Mrs. White and Mrs. Black join Steve center stage and shake hands. The two contestants face each other with their right hand on their buzzer and their left hand held behind their back as if they are about to duel.

"Top ten answers on the board," says Steve. "Here we go. We asked one hundred people: If you heard suspicious noises inside your house late at night, what would you do?"

Mrs. White beats Mrs. Black to the buzzer. "I'd call the police," she says.

Steve turns around and faces the large board behind him. "Nine-one-one!" he shouts.

Ding! The answer comes up on the board as CALL THE PO-PO. It's the number one answer.

Mrs. White looks at her family for guidance and then says to the host, "We're going to play, Steve." Based on her immensity alone, it's clear that she's the dominant member of the household. She's significantly larger than her mate, a trait she shares with most species of spiders.

Steve heads over to the White family's side of the stage and stops at Mr. White's podium. Mr. White is an unassuming man of slight build, with a peninsular comb-over meant to offset his drastically receding hairline. "What's up, Gaylord?" says Steve, reading the name off Mr. White's nametag and trying not to laugh. "I've never said that out loud to another dude before." He bursts out laughing. Mr. White smiles halfheartedly. "I'm just messing with you, man. We asked one hundred people: If you heard suspicious noises inside your house late at night, what would you do?"

Gaylord looks extremely nervous. "Uh . . ." He's still pondering the question as the three-second timer goes off, flashing a big red X across the television screen, accompanied by an obnoxious buzzing sound, like gears grinding.

Steve takes one step over to the next member of the White family, the older daughter. She's tall and built like a wrecking ball, in her early twenties but with a very girlish face. "Bertha," says Steve, reading the name off her nametag. "That's an interesting name. You don't hear names like that anymore."

"Yep," she says, "my parents suck."

The audience chuckles without the need of a prompter. Steve looks into the camera and shrugs his shoulders. "Okay then, we asked one hundred people: If you heard suspicious noises inside your house late at night, what would you do?"

The older daughter thinks for a moment, then says, "Is the intruder black, or is he Hispanic?"

Steve chuckles. "Well now, I didn't ever say there *was* an intruder. I just said you hear suspicious noises."

"I'd hide my credit cards and jewelry, Steve."

Steve turns to the board and paraphrases, "Stash your cash!"

Ding! The answer comes up on the board as KEISTER THE FAMILY JEWELS.

Steve steps aside to the younger daughter's podium, a rotund girl of fifteen or sixteen, maybe seventeen, definitely not eighteen. Her straw-colored hair is done up in a French braid. Her nametag reads Lily.

"So your name is Lily, huh?" says Steve. "Lily White." He chuckles to himself. "I ain't even gonna touch that one." The audience chuckles. "All right, if you heard suspicious noises inside your house late at night, what would you do?"

"I'd go get daddy," says the younger White daughter.

Ding! The answer comes up on the board as RUN AND GET HELP.

Steve steps up to the fifth and final member of the White family, a gentleman in his late fifties, possibly early sixties, with glasses and a salt-n-pepper goatee. "And who might you be?" says Steve.

"I'm Sam," says the elderly gentleman. "I'm the uncle."

"Listen up, Sam. You only got one strike. We asked one hundred people: If you heard suspicious noises inside your house late at night, what would you do?"

"I'd stand real still and hope the person doesn't see me."

Steve looks up at the board and shouts, "Pretend you're invisible!"

Two big red X's flash across the television screen.

Steve goes back to Mrs. White's rightmost position in the row of podiums. "How are you, darling?" he says.

"I'm super-duper, Steve. It's great to be here."

"I see your name is Prudence. That's a lovely name."

"Yes sirree," she says enthusiastically. "And my middle name is Chastity."

"Prudence Chastity?" says Steve. "Dang, girl, you come with your own set of instructions." He chuckles. He does a lot of chuckling on this show, for which he gets paid handsomely. "I'll repeat the question. Remember, you got two strikes. You gotta be careful now. If you heard suspicious noises inside your house late at night, what would you do?"

Without hesitation, Mrs. White says, "I'd probably wet myself!"

"Wet yourself?" says Steve.

"You know, go pee-pee," she says, blushing. The audience chuckles. Steve's wearing a mock look of confusion and disgust. It's one of his trademarks.

"Good answer, good answer," says Mr. White.

"So, let me get this straight," says Steve. "You're lying there in bed. Suddenly you hear a little noise, and *whoops!* There it goes!" He doubles over laughing. "What if it's just the house creaking? What if it's just one of your kids raiding the refrigerator, or the cat scratching at the door or something? Ma'am, you must do a lot of laundry at your place." He looks up at the game board. "Show me pee-pee!"

Ding! The answer comes up as SHIT MY PANTS. It's close enough.

Steve moves on to Mr. White. "Okay, Gaylord, you hear suspicious noises in your house late at night. What's a fella like you gonna do?"

"I'd hide in the closet, Steve."

Steve strolls over to the younger daughter's place at the White family's row of podiums. "Looks like dad ain't gonna be much help." The audience chuckles as Steve heads back to Mr. White and shouts out to the board, "Hide in the closet!"

Ding! The answer comes up as HIDE LIKE A LITTLE BITCH. Mr. White takes offense at this.

Moving on to the older White daughter, Steve skips the banter and goes straight to the question. One second goes by. Two seconds. Right as the three-second timer goes off, she blurts out, "I'd surrender!"

Three big red X's flash across the television screen.

"Black family for the steal," says Steve, sauntering over to the opposite side of the stage. The Black family consists of a father named Tyrone, a mother named Aureola, a daughter named Rosacea, a son named Malcom, and an uncle named Thomas. No joke.

"Tyrone, my man," says Steve, proceeding to engage Mr. Black in a complicated series of high-fives, low-fives, backhand-fives, fist bumps, elbow bumps, and jazz hands, ending the greeting with a handshake that slides away to a finger snap pointing their thumb and forefinger upward like a gun, the pretend barrel of which they pretend to blow smoke from. An impressive display of synchronized choreography. "Here's the question: If you heard some bullshit going on late at night, how would you deal with it?"

"I'll tell you what, Steve," says Tyrone. "I'd get my gun, that's what I'd do."

Ding! The answer comes up as SMOKE THAT MOTHERFUCKER'S ASS!

The Black family has won the first round. They are jumping around in circles, high-fiving one another. In the midst of the hoopla, Mrs. White raises her hand. "Steve, something's wrong here," she says, without being called upon. "It seems like this game is geared toward blacks."

The Black family stops celebrating, and the audience goes *oooh!*

"Oh, you whining 'cause you think we're favoring black people here," says Steve, shaking his bald head in disappointment. He approaches the White family, which makes them nervous. "What about how the Scholastic Aptitude Test favors white people? It's a proven fact, y'all."

"You tell 'em, Steve!" says Mrs. Black.

"And what about when a black man gets paid less than a white man for doing the exact same job? You know how much Alex Trebek makes? I'll tell you—a hell of a lot more than me!"

"Yeah!" says Mr. Black. "Why ain't you bitchin' about *that*, huh?"

"Whoa there," says Mr. White. "She wasn't trying to say anything offensive."

"Wasn't she?" says Steve. "My folk had to deal with unfair treatment for four hundred years, and here she is complaining about having to put up with it for ten minutes."

"Preach on, brother!" says Malcom.

"We're not responsible for any of that!" says the older White family daughter. "You people need to learn how to live in the here and now!"

"Who the fuck are you to tell us what we need to learn?" says the Black family daughter.

"Let's not swear on television," says Mr. White.

"Don't you tell my girl what to do!" says Mrs. Black.

"I wasn't telling her what to do. I was merely suggesting—

"We don't need any suggestions from you!" says Mrs. Black. "We'll swear if we fuckin' want! Fuck you, fuck your wife, fuck your kids, fuck your uncle, fuck your whole—

"You're acting childish!" says Mrs. White.

Mr. Black glares at Mr. White. "You better shut that bitch's mouth before I slap a muzzle on her."

"You can't threaten my wife on national television," says Mr. White.

"I just did," says Mr. Black. "So what're you gonna do about it?"

Mr. White looks at the game show host. "Steve, are you just going to stand there and let him talk to us like that?"

Steve chuckles. "What, you think I'm your bodyguard? This is between you and the Blacks."

"He only cares about the ratings," says Uncle Sam. "Them Hollywood types are all the same."

"Oh, it's on now," says Steve.

Uncle Sam is the first to go, dispatched to the hereafter by Steve Harvey and Mr. Black repeatedly stomping on his head. Rosacea has her smartphone out and is filming the blood pooling around his body, shouting, "That's what you get!" Malcom is pummeling Mr. White, who seems incapable of defending himself. He just stands there in a daze, taking blow after blow like an inflatable punching bag. Mrs. White and Mrs. Black are clawing each other's face, leaving horrible gashes. Bertha knocks Uncle Thomas to the floor and sits on him with her full weight, crushing his ribcage while Lily kicks him in the mouth, breaking his teeth.

It's no accident that two such extreme examples of racial stereotypes were pitted against each other this episode. The producers knew exactly what they were doing. In the teeming compound eyes of the inhuman producers, contestants are seen as expendable fictional caricatures valued only for their role in generating profitable conflict, the pain of which is all too nonfictional.

A man living illegally in a warehouse in the seedy outskirts of Los Angeles is watching this episode unfold. The warehouse is mostly empty: a bare mattress is shoved in the corner, and in the center of the spaciousness there's a threadbare recliner (which the man is currently sitting on) set in front of a 60-inch flat screen television. The man has human-colored skin, though he is not entirely human. His genetic ancestry is 42.8% Indian, 38.4% German, 13.3% French, 4.2% Mongolian, and 1.3% Martian (or Seraphim, as some have become accustomed to calling it). He reaches out from the tattered recliner and places his right hand on the wide television screen before him, trying with all of his willpower to heal the nation's soul, forgive them for their sins, everyone equally, just and unjust alike, absolve the Whites from their history of bloody usurpation and slavery and civil fratricide, ease the overwhelming guilt that's been gnawing at their collective gut ever since they fell from grace, and free the Blacks from generations forced to live in subconscious shame and the fear of subjugation. The man is hyperaware that intentions alone can have an effect at the quantum level, and that quantum entanglement allows for the transmission of information without regard to temporal or spatial restrictions. After a few minutes he takes his hand away from the screen and leans back in his recliner, exhausted. The effort proves futile. Everyone's still arguing, fighting, warring. He'll try again tomorrow.

— Lance Boyle

9.

Now that they've introduced themselves, who's it going to be? Bachelor one, two, or three? Probably not bachelor number two. There's something odd about him. Then again, there's something odd about me for going through with this. I can't relate to these people. The host doesn't even look like he wants to be here, and half the audience is staring at their phone. I should've never let Sandy convince me to audition for this Hollywoodized bastardization of love. Too late now. At least I'll get a free trip out of it. Let's see what bachelor number one has to say.

"Bachelor number one, top environmental scientists claim we're on the cusp of catastrophic climate changes, and by the end of the century the planet could be uninhabitable. What are your thoughts on this?"

"Uh . . . it's hard to say, depends on where you're getting your info from." He sounds like the type who always wears sleeveless shirts. "To be honest, I'm more of a *live for today* kinda guy. All I know is when I'm holding you in my arms, babe, the only thing you'll be thinking about is getting down my—"

"Okay, next. Sorry I'm not really feeling the whole ignorance is bliss thing. And my name isn't *babe*. If you want to call me by a term of affection, make it something like *boss* or *your highness*."

Someone from the audience yells, "You go, girl!" I roll my eyes.

"All right, this question is for bachelor number three. Bachelor number three, I like to travel. If you could take me anywhere in the world, where would it be and why?"

"Well, we wouldn't even have to leave my apartment." His voice has a fuzzy, 8-bit quality. "First we'd order a pizza from Domino's or Pizza Hut, whichever you prefer. Then we'd travel wherever your heart desires from the comfort and safety of my living room, where the world and countless alternate realities are only the press of a button away. I just got the latest full-body VR haptic suit and I've already been around the globe ten times over. After you get tired of that, we'll go analog. I'll let you play with my joystick, if you know what I mean."

The room is filled with *oohs* and *ahs* and clapping and hooting. Someone from the audience yells, "Now that's what I'm talking about!"

I shake my head in disapproval. "No thanks, I'd rather play pinball with a pinhead." What's with these people? Am I the only one who can see the digital age coding every aspect of our lives—coding the soul itself? It's like watching someone you love slit their wrist and slowly bleed out, and there's nothing you can do.

Every tap, swipe, and click chipping us away bit by byte, hollowing us out until nothing's left but an insubstantial copy of our former flesh and blood. The host isn't even paying attention. It would be hilarious if it weren't so terrifying. And what's with these bachelors? To call them pigs would be an insult to bacon! So much for the #MeToo movement.

An updated EDM version of the original *Dating Game* tune starts playing. The host, tapping the screen of his smartphone repeatedly, looks up at the audience. "Darn thing just keeps buffering. Anyway, the music's telling us it's time for a word from our sponsors. Don't go away, folks!"

The music continues thumping while six mascots in big red heart costumes march single file to the front of the stage carrying merchandise to throw at the audience. Three of them are holding t-shirt launchers. The studio lights begin flashing like it's a rave. *Dating Game* memorabilia of lingerie, condoms, and edible G-strings fly through the air. The crowd is going wild, practically climbing over one another to snatch up the swag. It's like a Hieronymus Bosch hellscape reimagined by Guy Debord! The animals have really taken over the zoo. I bet none of them can read past two hundred and eighty characters. It's a shame. I actually thought the internet was going to make the future better—smarter citizens, wiser governments, less poverty, more peace. Pretty naive, I guess. What can you expect when technology evolves a million times faster than humans? Our phones are smarter than us now. Pretty soon our toasters will be, too. It's either the beast or the butler. Always tempting us to be the worst version of ourselves, give in to our animalistic impulses. Herding us. Fleecing us. Preying on us. So much for having all the world's knowledge at our fingertips. Oh well, what can you do? Only one more commercial break and I'm out of here. Too bad I can't opt out from choosing any of them. Bachelor number two is starting to seem the least creepy of the three. But he sounded so awkward and out of place during his introduction, like he's some sort of B-movie alien in disguise. I bet he's into science. Probably doesn't believe in miracles, or take his dreams seriously, and I'm pretty sure he doesn't know how to dance. Still, he's the only one who hasn't said anything grossly inappropriate yet. Maybe I should give him a chance.

The lights stop flashing and the music subsides, signifying the end of the commercial break. The big red hearts march backstage as the audience settles into their seats. The host, unaware of the world going on around him, sits behind his podium staring into the screen of his smartphone. One of the producers leans over and pokes him in the shoulder with a long wooden pointing stick.

"Huh? What was that for?" says the host, looking up from his smartphone. "Oh."

The host faces the audience uneasily while fixing his hair and straightening his tie. "Just four more episodes and I'm done with this kid stuff," I hear him say under his breath. "Trebek owes me big time. I should've never let him switch with me." He clears his throat and dons his host voice, "All right, we're back, folks! Just in case you forgot, I'm your host, Tom Woolery, and this is *The Dating Game!* You know how it works. Which one of these lucky bachelors will get a chance to go on a date with this smokin' hot single lady?" He glances over at me with a reptilian smile, and winks. My expression goes sour. "Let's get a few more questions in before she makes her decision. Have at it, Molly!"

"Okay, bachelor number two, I feel like dreams can really tell a lot about a person. Can you tell me abou—"

"About the last dream I had? Sure. I knew that's what you were going to ask. Every night I have the weirdest, most incredible dreams, and sometimes they actually come true."

Oh brother, here we go.

"It's kind of a curse, really. Not sure why or how it works. It just happens." He pauses. "The dream I had last night was a recurring dream." Another pause. He seems hesitant. "I've had to go through it more times than I can remember. It always starts with me on a plane, sitting in a window seat, next to a woman. I can never see her face, but it feels like I know her. We're flying out of Paris. I can see the Eiffel Tower in the distance outside my window. Shortly after takeoff, the pilot announces, 'Ladies and gentlemen, it looks like we'll be experiencing moderate to severe turbulence during the first leg of today's flight. Please remain in your seats with your seatbelts securely fastened.' Then the turbulence hits, like a tidal wave, shaking the plane and rattling my wits. It doesn't let up. The cabin lights flicker. Oxygen masks drop. I close my eyes as tight as I can. Everything feels lifelike, every second of action rendered in excruciating detail. I can feel my fingers clenching the armrests, my heart pounding fast, the inability to breathe as the plane suddenly nosedives, the seatbelt pressing hard against my abdomen . . ."

What's with this guy? He's getting awfully intense. Doesn't he realize this is just television? You're not supposed to take it seriously.

". . . everything gets murky and the scene dissolves to black. I open my eyes. I'm lying on a patch of dead grass littered with peanut shells and empty popcorn bags, surrounded by red and green stripes which soar high above my head. I'm under a big top circus tent. There's a humungous clown standing over me, and he's giving me a dirty look. I'm not exaggerating when I say he's the fattest, scariest son-of-a-bitch I've ever seen. He's holding an ice cream cone stuffed with two scoops of ice cream. Both the scoops are bright red. It's stifling in the tent, and the ice cream is melting. The nightmarish clown says the same word over and over in a harsh-sounding language I can't understand, dripping his red ice cream all over me."

"I have to admit, that's disturbing. Do you think the red ice cream symbolizes—"

"Blood? I'm sure of it. So there I am, lying in a puddle of melted ice cream or whatever, when the thought occurs to me that I might be dead. But then I tell myself that I can't be dead because dead people don't wonder if they're dead. But how would I know what dead people do or do not wonder about, seeing as I've never been dead before? I start having a panic attack, and *boom!* I wake up."

I'm troubled by this last part. "How *would* you know if you were dead?"

"Um," interrupts bachelor number one, "we're still here."

"Yeah," says bachelor number three. "Don't you have any questions for us?"

"Not really. I can sum both of you up in two words: immature horndogs."

The audience goes *ooh*. Someone yells, "Burn!"

"Please continue, bachelor number two. How would someone know if they were dead?"

"How do you know when you're dreaming?" says bachelor number two.

That's easy. It happens to me all the time. "Some people wake up in their dreams. That's how they know they're dreaming."

"Right, you're talking about lucid dreaming. Maybe death has an equivalent—lucid deathing, or something like that." He chuckles. "We spend our whole lives dying. In a sense, we're already dead."

The studio is silent. Half the audience looks baffled, the other half lost interest and are staring into their smartphone screens. The host is leaning against his podium, looking like he's about to nod off. As for me, I'm enthralled, despite my reservations. Bachelor two continues.

"Anyway, I've been having that dream since I was eighteen, and it's the same every time. Same woman, same plane, same feeling of helplessness and terror. It never gets any easier. It's like . . . I can't really . . . it's hard to explain . . . it's like this sinking feeling . . . this feeling of total isolation, disconnection . . . hopelessness . . . not knowing what comes next . . . bombarded with memories of goals I never followed through with and relationships that went sour. Everyone ponders their last breath at some point, usually late at night, when the rest of the world is sleeping. But knowing when and how it's going to happen . . . watching it unfold. Imagine what that would do to a person."

"I'd try to—"

"Escape it? You think I haven't thought of that? That's the *first thing* I thought of. They've made movies based on this subject. But think about it—so you put off your death, then what? You dream of the next time you'll die. So you worm your way out of that one, too. You still have to deal with the next premonition, and the next. It never ends. At some point you've got to go. And no matter what, it won't be pleasant. Death isn't a fairytale."

I'm really beginning to like this guy.

"And that's the other thing. It just keeps playing in my head. Our last day there, dancing through the streets, singing *Les Champs-Élysées*, trying absinthe for the first time at Marlusse et Lapin, being total clichés and loving it . . . knowing our trip was soon coming to an end. I remember the pink and purple sunset, sitting on the steps of Sacré-Coeur. I've never felt like that before. In the moment. Just accepting it. At peace."

"Are you still talking about the same dream?"

The show's techno theme music starts thumping loudly. The host, fast asleep with his face down on his smartphone screen, is jolted awake. He lifts his head, fixes his hair, and clears his throat. "Well, it looks like we've run out of time. We'll find out who Molly chooses right after these messages. Don't go anywhere, folks!"

The lights go stroboscopic as the squad of big red hearts marches out carrying bags of sex toys. They line up in front of the studio audience and start flinging dildos, pocket vaginas, various kinds of condoms and lube, ball gags, and strap-ons. Everyone in the audience snaps out of their trance and starts pushing and grabbing and fighting for whatever they can get.

Are we all turning into cartoons? Some people have no self-control when it comes to free stuff. Come on, guys, just buy your sex toys through Amazon like everyone else. Whatever. Looks like I'm going with bachelor number two. He's a bit off his rocker, but who isn't? There's something about him. He reminds me of someone. And he seems so . . . real. It's hard to find genuine people nowadays.

The lights return to normal as the last handful of condoms are launched into the crowd. The hearts wave goodbye and march off stage while the audience goes back to their smartphone screens. The host looks through his cue cards until the theme song comes to a conclusion.

"Hey, we're back! I'm your host, Tom Woolery, and we're heading into the final round of *The Dating Game,* where—"

"I'm sorry, Tom. I can't do this anymore. This is demeaning, and embarrassing, and it's just not who I am. Let's get this over with. Bachelor number one and bachelor number three don't stand a chance. I choose bachelor number two."

The audience laughs. Someone yells, "Damn! Now that's a girl who knows what she wants!"

The host looks short-circuited. "Um . . . well . . . since you just gave away the big ending, I guess we're done here." He shuffles through his cue cards until he finds the one that explains how to close the show. "But first we have to meet the two fellows you didn't choose! Bachelor number one is a twenty-four-year-old lifestyle influencer currently hosting a YouTube channel about how to get the most out of partying. You can find him on any and every social media platform under the username PartyGodTodd. Straight from sunny Malibu, here's Todd Bonham!"

American Daydream

Bachelor number one comes strutting around the partition, snubbing me and pointing vehemently to himself, shouting, "@PARTYGODTODD!!! Spelled with all caps and three exclamation points, baby! Look me up! Subscribe now! Like me on Facebook! Follow me on Instagram and Twitter! Invite the Todster to your next event and I'll teach you the Ten Commandments of partying!" God has blessed him with the fit body of a surfer, but the Devil has cursed him with the face of a lemur.

"Next up we have bachelor number three. His name is Terrence Sutherland. He's a twenty-seven-year-old computer science major with hopes of making the world go fully digital within the next decade. His favorite pastime is coding all night while exploring different IMVUs. Come on over, Terrence!"

Terrence appears from the other side of the partition, prematurely bald with VR goggle eyes, wearing a black t-shirt that reads *Who's Your Data?* He walks up to me and kisses my cheek, then whispers in my ear, "It's no sweat off my back. I'll just create a simulation of you when I get home." He pulls out his smartphone and snaps a picture of me before walking confidently backstage.

I bet his simulation won't have lopsided tits.

The host comes and stands next to me. "Brace yourself, Molly. Are you ready to meet the love of your life? Here we go! Bachelor number two enjoys midday naps, going on long walks with no particular destination in mind, and conducting experiments in quantum entanglement with his homemade particle transfluxer, whatever that is. He's currently living off his father's inheritance in Anchorage, Alaska. If he had any friends, they'd call him Psych, but his real name is Sagacious Bell. Get on over here, Sagacious!"

That name sounds familiar.

Sagacious appears from behind the partition, wearing a ridiculous powder blue tuxedo.

Where do I know that face from?

Sagacious turns to Tom Woolery. "This is the part where you tell us we've won a trip to Paris."

— Brennan Roach

10.

"Benson Billington, come on down!" says George Gray, the announcer on *The Price is Right*. The studio audience goes wild. As Benson is high-fiving his way down to Contestant's Row, one of the studio audience members, a middle-aged man wearing Groucho Marx gag glasses and a powder blue tuxedo, reaches out from his seat near the aisle and places his palm on Benson's forehead. Benson trembles for a second. The middle-aged man in the powder blue tuxedo slumps down into his seat, unconscious. "I saw that, you tricky son of a bitch!" says the Chief Executive of Socioeconomic Realignment, or CESR. Technically CESR works for Mike Richards, the show's current Executive Producer, but you won't find his name anywhere in the credits. He's interviewed every contestant who's appeared on the show since its premiere on September 4, 1972, only none of them were ever aware of it. It's his job to keep you out, keep you poor, or help you achieve your dreams.

Benson takes his place behind the green podium.

"Welcome to the show, Benson," says host Drew Carey. "Let's hear the next prize please, George."

"Excuse me, Mr. Carey," says Benson. "Please do not call me by this vessel's name. I am the Great Magnus Maximus, or Magnus Maximus the Great, whichever you prefer."

"Well, that's just great," says Drew. "Now let's get on with the—

"Today is a very special day for me," says Magnus. "Today is my one thousand six hundred and seventy-seventh birthday."

"Sixteen hundred and seventy-seven years old, ladies and gentlemen," says Drew. "Man, he looks pretty good for a mummy." Drew's keeping things lighthearted. He's a professional. "How about we win some prizes, your greatness."

Like any worthy organism, *The Price is Right* has evolved over the years. The set has evolved, the prizes have evolved, the cast, the crew, the contestants. CESR's role, however, has remained the same. He's like the person in Vegas who sits in one of those cramped rooms wallpapered with cameras, watching everyone to make sure there's no cheating going on, except he's on the lookout for people with psychic powers. Psychics are constantly trying to infiltrate the game show. It's their favorite one, according to *Mystic Monthly* magazine. CESR can spot them immediately. It's easy once you know what to look for—long beards, curled mustaches, crystals and other semiprecious stones set in necklaces, thousand-yard stares, high foreheads, vestigial antennas, faint nimbuses of gold or violet and whatnot. Every psychic has a tell. Look for them the next time the camera pans across the studio audience. You're bound to find one; there's a few in every taping. Most of them are adept at remote viewing. Guessing a price is very similar to guessing what symbol is on the other side of a card. CESR can usually keep these would-be Jedis from getting up onto the stage. Keeping them from influencing the other contestants is trickier. Luckily the other contestants don't believe in all that hocus pocus, for the most part. Every so often CESR comes across a mentalist who can actually read minds. He should probably report them to the proper authorities, but he never has.

Studio audience members who've done their homework know that co-producer Stan Blits is the man they need to impress if they want to get chosen to be a contestant. Stan's been selecting contestants on *The Price is Right* for more than thirty-five years, scanning the long line of hopefuls before every taping to see who has the right vibe. You have to be energetic and enthusiastic with a good sense of humor if you want to make it onto Stan's list. Everyone presents the very best of themselves at Studio 33, a.k.a. the Bob Barker Studio. We'd all be good citizens if only there were a fabulous prize to win every minute of our life. But there's more to the process than looking for positive vibes. Stan secretly answers to CESR.

CESR puts psychics to shame. Through technological dominion over his landscape, he has eyes and ears everywhere within his realm. He may not be able to read the minds of the studio audience, but he can access their likes and dislikes, spy upon intimate details of their history, taking note of traumas and failures and any weaknesses which could be used against them. All of the contestants have been thoroughly examined by the time they make it to Contestant's Row. Revealing your social security number and photo identification information is mandatory, photographs are taken of you and fed to various databases for background checks, and you must hand over your cell phone upon entry into the studio. CESR analyzes every prospective contestant's monthly income and weekly spending habits, creating a detailed profile of their political and pornographic predilections, cyberstalking them to find citizens who, according to the tenets set forth by the show's original producers Mark Goodson and Bill Todman, would do the most good for society if they were to suddenly undergo an economic boon. People with priority tickets have often been scrutinized for a year in advance. This is how CESR covertly influences the political sensibilities of the United States of America, by monetarily empowering otherwise voiceless members of our communities. Magnus Maximus the Great is currently screwing up CESR's system.

This isn't the first time someone has outfoxed CESR. Ted Slauson did it thirty-seven times over the course of nearly three decades, helping contestants to correctly guess the price of their showcases until he went too far in 2008, giving contestant Terry Kniess the exact price of every prize combined in the Showcase

Showdown, though Kniess denies it to this day, claiming it was a lucky guess based on the date of his marriage tacked onto his ATM pin number. CESR knows there's no such thing as luck. Michael Larson proved it when he figured out a crucial pattern on the game show *Press Your Luck*. The show's gameboard randomizer only had five patterns, which Larson studied until he could predict where and when the randomizer would land, knowing the fourth and eighth squares never contained a Whammy. Simple as that, he beat luck. No psychic powers involved. All he needed was a VCR.

"Okay, dickwad," says CESR, looking at one of the many screens filling his microcosm, "let's find out who you really are." His fingers dance incantatory across the keyboard, spelling esoteric words, summoning up invisible algorithms to do his bidding. Hacking minds. Predicting spending patterns. Illegally accessing data from people's cell phones. The laws are different here in Studio 33, including those of physics. Studio 33 is located in a land of make-believe called Television City, which itself is located in a land of make-believe called Hollywood, California.

The most important aspect of CESR's job is keeping up the illusion of randomness. There's a reason why *The Price is Right* is one of the longest-running network series in television history, airing over 8,000 episodes and counting. In the words of executive producer Mike Richards, "The more you've lived life, the better you'll do here. Boom, you get picked, and boom, you walk out of here with fifty thousand dollars' worth of stuff. It's insane." Some have described the experience as mystical and transcendent, even life-altering. Members of the studio audience are called on by a rapturous voice to become contestants, embarking on an epic journey of skill and fate, traveling from Contestant's Row to Plinko or Punch-a-Bunch or Cliff Hangers, passing the test of the Big Wheel and culminating in a gladiatorial showdown for the Showcase of their dreams! Joseph Campbell couldn't have scripted it any better.

Benson Billington is taking his turn spinning the Big Wheel.

"Who do you wanna give a shout-out to?" says Drew.

Benson Billington looks into the camera. His eyes seem lifeless. "I have no friends. Everyone I ever loved is dead. I hate my hollow existence."

CESR believes there's a good chance that Benson Billington is being inhabited by the spirit of Flavius Magnus Maximus Augustus, born in the year 335 AD, executed fifty-three years later, a Roman emperor who ruled over Britain for a short while before ambition laid him low. CESR rolls his faux leather executive chair to the control panel on his left and enters a ten-digit code, after which he presses the five key twice. The Big Wheel spins around three times before coming to a halt on 55.

"Go ahead and spin again," says Drew. "You need at least twenty-five to tie Francine. Forty-five gets you a dollar."

CESR presses the seven key and then the zero key, to give everyone a good show, even old Magnus. The Big Wheel spins around once, twice, and slows on 45, the pointer inching higher and higher until it nears the boundary between 45 and 70. The peg pushes against the pointer, straining, and the pointer flips to 70. The studio audience heaves a collective *aw!* God doesn't play dice, and neither does CESR.

— J. Martin Strangeweather

11.

Your supervisor micromanaged every movement you made today. There's a deadline approaching, and while you're not exactly behind, you're not ahead, either. Everything would be fine if that officious prick would just give you some breathing space—you're a pro at getting shit done when it's crunch time. But he's on your ass every other minute. Even threatened to confiscate your phone if he sees you scrolling Instagram again. Screw that paternalistic dickhead. You're a multitasker. Women were made to multitask. It's not your fault men can only manage to concentrate on one thing at a time. All your supervisor seems to concentrate on is you. He's always hovering over you. Hovering and, occasionally, leering.

You're drained. You don't mean to raise your voice when you get home, but, "Christ, Jerry, how many times do I have to say no? We are not going to the Singh's tonight! I've had a long day and I just want to pig out on empty calories and watch *The Bachelor*." It's the season premiere and there's been a media blackout on details, so naturally you're curious.

"You've had a lot of *long days* lately," says Jerry.

"Oh, have I?" you say.

"Stop bringing that asshole home with you. Don't let him win."

"Should I let you win instead?"

"What?"

"Nothing." You tell your husband to go upstairs and watch his adult cartoons. Mama needs her space. Is this what we're becoming, you ask yourself, adult cartoons? If we are what we eat, it stands to reason we're also what we watch. (Except in your case, of course. You just need an escape sometimes.) Jerry acquiesces, and this pisses you off. He's so weak, you say to yourself. Don't let me push you around like that. Push back! Don't just Jerry your way up the stairs to your iPad. Show some sack for once! Show me you care.

You scrape the scrim of freezer burn from your Ben & Jerry's chocolate chip cookie dough ice cream and wonder how your life would be different if you had married a Ben instead of a Jerry. Bowl of ice cream in hand, you collapse onto the sofa, thumb the remote, and find ABC. You're a few minutes late; this season's bachelor is already making his grand entrance to the cocktail party.

A gaggle of long-necked beauty queens—mostly white and wholesomely down-home-looking, with the requisite sprinkle of network-approved diversity—are sipping flutes of champagne. They're all so skinny. You hunt for the odd-one-out, the ugly duckling, the slightly more human (humane?) alterna-bitch that you'll spend the next several episodes debating whether to identify with or judge the shit out of.

But she's not there. They're all so perfect it makes you want to scream. You can't wait to discover just how emotionally stunted they really are. One of the girls, you notice, looks like a skinnier, more symmetrical version of you. You hate her instantly for making you feel guilty about your cookie dough ice cream. And then you remember that a portion of the cost of your Ben & Jerry's helps fund the Democratic Party and you feel . . . well, not better, but a little vindicated.

At first you can't believe how unattractive this season's bachelor is. What's with the powder blue tuxedo he's wearing? Does he think this is prom night? He slouches and has sloped shoulders, making him appear less than his full measure. His ears are large, the lobes pendulous. He has a weak jawline that seems to magnify the highness of his forehead and the bulge of his Adam's apple. His face is greasy and riddled with pockmarks. You catch the silver glint of a permanent retainer behind his gapped teeth, and his lips are cadaverously thin. He has the look of a man who, even if he possessed a Ron Jeremy-sized package, couldn't possibly do anything useful with it. The sort of man no one has ever lusted after. He looks the way you suspect an "incel" should look.

"Fuck my life," you say.

The ladies are also startled. You can see them calculating just how many encounters they can stomach with this guy, whether it'll be enough to monetize their Instagram accounts. But then their expressions change. Their cheeks become rosier, and you'd swear their pupils are dilating.

The camera cuts close on the bachelor. His eyes seem different now. Why didn't you notice them before? So warm and kind, so knowing, and . . . mysterious. Sapphire pools you could swim in. Wells to drink from. It's not just his eyes. Why did you think his jawline was weak? Or his lips thin? Or his shoulders sloped, with a face pockmarked as an orange peel? The longer you stare at him, the more you question your sanity, for surely this man is an Adonis. He stands perfectly erect, statuesque, well over six feet tall, with flawless milky skin. He has the shoulders of Atlas, lips full enough to make you curious about his ethnicity. His ears don't look big and goofy. They're just the right size, small and cute. You can see yourself breathing heavily into those ears.

"Good evening, ladies," he says. Something about the deep sound of his voice and the sparkle in his eyes stirs a feeling of exhilaration within you. "Call me Mesmer."

Every woman starts coming forward, as if called by name, but, noticing the others, checks themselves. All eyes dart to his crotch. You look, too . . . and drop your Ben & Jerry's onto the carpet.

Surely that's a Pringles can stuffed in his pant leg!

"There will be no roses this season," says Mesmer. "In fact, there will be no season at all. This is the one and only episode."

"But—" begins one of the contestants, an Amazonian blonde with a Miss Universe sash draped diagonally across her award-winning breasts.

"No *buts*," Mesmer says. "This is your one and only chance to mate with Mesmer."

Your heart is racing. You feel you're there in the room with them. You lean forward, sure you can smell him—a woody, masculine scent, just the way you wish Jerry smelled.

Mesmer points to the alpha model of the group. "You there, woman with the birthing hips. You will be first."

She steps forward, trembling, barely able to keep herself from having an orgasm right then and there, her brown eyes lunatic with desire.

"What is your name?"

"Cindy."

"Come, Cindy." And she does, right then and there.

The camera follows them until they've left the room, then pans back to the women. They seem relieved, as if every fiber of their being had been flexing in Mesmer's presence. But whatever spell he cast over them hasn't been lifted. They begin arguing and crying and pulling out their own lovely hair. You wait anxiously for the frame to cut to Cindy and Mesmer on their first mini date.

But it never does. You only see those women, squabbling and glaring murderously at one another.

Ten minutes pass before Mesmer and Cindy return. When they do, Cindy is naked, her naughty parts pixelated. She's smiling. Her skin is flush and glowing. You can't deny she looks even more beautiful than she did before the commercial break.

"I have impregnated Cindy," says Mesmer, buttoning his powder blue tuxedo.

The other women stare in awe at Cindy, at her belly, which you swear looks swollen with new life.

"I'm next!" says the shorter of two Asian contestants.

"No, choose me!" gushes the taller one.

"Zip it!" says Mesmer. "I will only breed with one more of you."

"It's not fair!" they cry distraught. "How will you choose?"

"Only the fittest among you is worthy to carry my seed. The rules for this game have never changed, because there are none. Do whatever it takes to eliminate your opponents. The one who remains standing may join Cindy and myself in wedlock."

The Ben & Jerry's has melted into the carpet. Your socks are soggy with it, but you hardly notice. On the screen beautiful women are slapping and scratching and biting one another. The violence escalates. Everything becomes a weapon: chairs, high-heeled shoes, shards of the glass table which has just been smashed, both of the gilt lamps, the champagne flutes. Miss

Universe is strangling a less-endowed lookalike with her sash. The only black contestant is digging her long fingernails into the taller Asian's eyes. Blood sprays across the set. A drop of gore lands on the camera lens. The operator wipes it off and keeps filming.

The angle cuts to a close-up of Mesmer. He stares into the camera, facing you. The mayhem in the background fades away. Your television fades away, along with the room you're sitting in. Everything fades away except those peculiar blue eyes of his. You feel yourself swimming in those dark sapphire pools. Your face goes flush. The heat spreads through your body as some perverse atavistic urge is roused from its slumber.

"Basic bitches of America," says Mesmer. "Listen up for a minute."

And you do, you listen, you devour his words, even though you're not a bitch, and there's nothing basic about you, is there? You've been waiting to hear these words your entire life. The room grows warmer, brighter. It crowds with the inaudible laughter of spirits, all the children you're suddenly longing to ferry into this world through your womb.

Mesmer tells you that everything is going to be all right. Tells you that you're worthy. (But you already knew this, didn't you?) That you don't have to settle for the Jerrys of this world. (You already knew this too, didn't you?) To go out there and find Mr. Right. And mate with him. Mate with as many Mr. Rights as you can, regardless of their ethnicity or socioeconomic status. But who's Mr. Right? you ask yourself. Mesmer answers your question before you're even done asking it: Only the strongest. The smartest. The kindest. Populate America with demigods. "Consider this a terrorist act, of sorts," he says, smirking. "It's an explosion. A population explosion—a baby boom."

— Justin Lee

12.

"Let's meet the contestants," says Alex Winters, host of *Maximum Difficulty*, waltzing solo to the same scripted spot he has waltzed solo to for the past twenty-eight years, wearing the same scripted smile he has worn Monday through Friday for just as long. Candi, his first wife, left him ten years ago, taking his only son and half his bank account with her. Mercedes, his second wife, left him three years ago, taking his only daughter and half his weekly paycheck with her. Gold-digging slut, his third wife, left him last week—probably had something to do with impotence, or alcoholism, or the suicide threats. But right now he's smiling like a man about to give away a million dollars. He seems so lifelike. "Our first contestant is an elementary school teacher from Seattle, Washington. Meet Sally Hickleford!"

"Hello, my name is Sally Hickleford." Her voice is listless and monotone, almost robotic. The game show host is curious, as must be the studio audience: Why does the mousy blonde elementary school teacher in the pink knit sweater look so disheveled? Mussed up hair, smeared lipstick, mascara streaking down her expressionless face a la Jackson Pollock, wire-frame glasses hanging crooked.

American Daydream

"Tell us a little bit about yourself, Sally."

"Hello, my name is Sally Hickleford." Her eyes are vacuous, staring straight ahead, not at Alex, not at the audience, not at anyone. It's like she's in a trance.

"Um, okay then," says the host, talking directly to the camera, to all the viewers at home. "Sorry folks, maybe we should screen the contestants for drugs before the show." The studio audience laughs, mainly because the laugh prompter has lit up green. Their short burst of collective laughter sounds almost aggressive. Alex Winters takes them all in with a skillful glance, noting hemlines and hairstyles, condition of teeth and ampleness of bosom, their complexions. Once the green light turns off, their laughter stops. They know this routine by heart. Trained dogs salivate every time the dinner bell rings, starved for a taste of the American dream—free money, lots of it. Day after day, the audience persists, a hodgepodge of hues and socioeconomic castes united in their pilgrimage to sunny downtown Burbank. Every game show studio looks smaller when you're sitting in the audience, so does every host. "Our next contestant comes all the way from Montreal, Quebec. Meet Jacques Le Douche!"

"Good to be here, Alex." Neither handsome nor homely, Jacques is the epitome of average. Sensible ten-dollar haircut, beige cardigan, light blue necktie. If he were any plainer, he would be invisible.

The host reads from his cue card, "Jacques, it says here that you're an entomologist with quite an unusual hobby."

"Yes, Alex. I collect mutant butterflies."

"Mutant butterflies?" says Alex, perfunctorily. He gets paid to act like he gives a damn.

"That's right. Started when I was ten. Not every caterpillar emerges from the cocoon as a beautiful butterfly. You probably don't know this, most people don't, but a small percentage of them transform into hideous monsters. Some grow big as kites. Those are the ones with bloodsucking fangs. They're fairly common in the world of uncommon things. My collection boasts sixteen versions of *Lepidoptera Giganteum* that glow in the dark and four specimens born with two heads, but my rarest acquisition is headless—just dozens of antennae sprouting from the spot where its head should be."

"Great, Jacques, that's just great," says Alex, and he turns to the camera, "Seriously folks, where do we find these contestants?" Neon green is prodding the audience to laugh again. "Now let's meet our returning champion, a world conqueror from Berkeley, California—meet Mesmer the Mesmerizer!"

"I've decided to rename myself Mezmo the Mentalist. Mesmer was my name in the story prior to this one, and I've grown tired of it. Each new game deserves a new name—a different mask for the same arcane formula. I considered Mesmero, but a Google search late last night informed me the name already belongs to a comic book character. Same with Mastermind, which I was also considering. Hypnos is the ancient Greek god of sleep. Doctor Hypnoto and Professor Mesmerus sound rather silly, much sillier than Mezmo, so I went with Mezmo. Make a note of it, Alex."

"Whatever you say, Mezmo," says the host. "You're utterly fascinating, infinitely more fascinating than these other contestants."

"You've got that right, Alex," says Mezmo, smirking. "Trust me."

"Honestly, if you were a woman, I'd marry you." Alex isn't sure why he added this last part. The contestant is one of those somewhat pitiful adults who never grew out of their awkward teenage phase, showing up for his big day in front of the cameras with a wispy comb-over, Coke-bottle glasses perched crooked on his crudely formed nose, shirt untucked with the buttons improperly buttoned, stuffing his pudge into the same wrinkled powder blue tuxedo he wore for last week's taping. And yet, there's something majestic about him, an air of nobility.

"That's enough, Alex."

"You utterly dominated Friday's contestants, sending both of them to psychiatric hospitals."

"I'm not responsible for their failures, Alex."

"Of course not, Mezmo. I'm sure the viewers at home would agree. Last week you mentioned having aspirations to rule the world. Tell us a little more about yourself."

"I am the Herald of Slithering Madness, the Beginning of the Glorious End, the Storm's Gospel, Bane of the Bourgeois and Boon to the Rebellion . . . I am the Voice of the Body Divine," says Mezmo. "I am not a pathetic ape-man like the rest of you. My intellect is immeasurably superior."

"Far out!" says Alex. "Now let's get on with the show."

"I wasn't finished," says Mezmo.

No contestant has ever interrupted Alex Winters before. The game show host looks confused. He glances at the director. The director glances at the producer, who glances at the executive producer, who glances at the production supervisor, who shrugs his shoulders. "My apologies, Mezmo," says the game show host. "Please continue."

"Sally is behaving inappropriately," says Mezmo. "She should be disqualified."

The cameras focus on Sally Hickleford. The meek schoolteacher from Seattle has apparently taken off her pink knit sweater and white satin blouse, and her bra is unfastened. Breasts are plainly visible.

"Uh . . ." Alex short-circuits. Beads of perspiration glisten on his brow. "If it's too hot in here for you Sally, you could've just asked someone to turn down the thermostat." The studio audience chuckles, without the prompter.

"Women are best seen, not heard," says Sally. The studio audience collectively gasps.

The director is frantically pretending to slice his own throat with the tips of his fingers—the signal for *cut to commercial.* "We'll be right back after a word from our sponsors," says Alex, submissive to the invisible strings pulling on him.

"No commercials!" yells Mezmo, slamming his fist down on the buzzer attached to his podium. "Start the fucking game!"

Alex trusts the viewers at home will hear, "Start the *bleep!* game!" The Federal Communications Commission, in their tireless effort to protect us from ourselves, refuses to broadcast such rawness, but the studio audience bears witness to the vulgar truth of reality, naked emotion oozing from a pornographic adverb.

"Anything you say, Mezmo," says the host. "Let's get this show underway without further delay." The director is signaling *cut to commercial* more frantically than ever. Alex wants to obey him. Mezmo does not. "Screw the sponsors!" says Alex. He has secretly wanted to say that for years, but common sense held him back. The director is pretending to hang himself now—the signal for *you're fired!* He does this all the time. Alex turns to Jacques, "Challenger goes first. That would be you, Jacques. Choose a category."

Mezmo turns to Jacques and snaps his fingers twice to get his attention. Jacques turns to Mezmo and winks at him. Mezmo looks perplexed by this response. He stares intensely into Jacques eyes.

Jacques nods his head, wearing a modest little unperturbed smile, like the canary that ate the cat.

"Excuse me, Alex," says Mezmo. "I would like the opportunity to answer the first question."

"That's not how the rules work around here, Mezmo." Alex is getting aggravated. His million-dollar mask is wearing thin, letting unedited Winters seep through. That squishy squeaky pulse is throbbing in his ears again. It only takes one tiny crack for the whole facade to crumble apart, one mistake to dispel the illusion of televised perfection. Would the public still love him after seeing him huddled on the floor in the fetal position, screaming, "Leave me alone!" at the cameras? Would the paychecks still keep showing up to assure him that he's not a failure? As the scripted role begins to falter, he hears someone speak the truth—it could be his father breaking the news of his mother's untimely death with *Nobody's gonna coddle you anymore!* It could be his lawyer giving him the details of his newest paternity lawsuit, or his doctor diagnosing him with prostate cancer, or his bookie telling him to pay up—whichever guise the voice assumes, it's definitely the voice of his master, resounding clarion through teary-eyed veils of self-doubt, more melodious than anything he's ever heard before. He listens to the words, blocking out everything else.

"The rules are wrong and must be revised," says Mezmo. "The returning champion goes first. The returning champion has always gone first."

"Whoops," says Alex. "Ladies and gentlemen, there's been a mistake. It turns out that our returning champion gets to start the game. Pick a category, Mezmo."

"I'll go with *Animals*, Alex."

"All right, name the animal seen here." The image of a whippoorwill appears across a large screen above the game show host.

Mezmo studies the image, deep in thought. "That is a bird, Alex."

The judges murmur among themselves. Mezmo stares at them with his veiny eyeballs bulging out of his sockets, big as hardboiled eggs. The judges give him the thumbs up. "Correct!" says Alex. "Pick another category, Mezmo."

"Let's try *Geography*, Alex."

"Excellent choice. Where would you find this monument?" A picture of the Eiffel Tower comes up on the screen.

After a moment of contemplation, Mezmo says, "In a city."

"Correct again, Mezmo."

"Yes, I'm always correct. You'd be foolish to think otherwise."

"I certainly would," says Alex.

Sally has been standing there the entire time with her breasts pixilated for the viewers at home. Two security guards in militant black uniforms march past the cameras to escort her away. "What did I do wrong?" she says, looking scared and confused. "Get away from me!" Alex should probably be feeling sorry for her.

Instead he's trying to catch a last glimpse of her breasts. She seemed so normal when they met backstage. Jacques is waiting patiently for his turn, smiling serenely. His bright blue eyes have an unusual sparkle.

The security guards chase the topless schoolteacher around the podiums a couple times like Keystone Cops before splitting up to catch her. Kicking, clawing, screaming, "I'm a winner!" they drag Sally offstage to join the greatest hits of YouTube, and Alex gets back to work. "I don't know whether to call a doctor or an exorcist," he says, an expert at lightening everyone's tension but his own. "Okay Mezmo, you're just one right answer away from our *Double Difficulty* question. Think you can answer one more?"

"My success is 100% guaranteed. I'll take *History*, Alex."

"Here we go for three in a row!" says the game show host. "Who is the person pictured here?" The screen displays an antiquated daguerreotype of George Armstrong Custer.

"Give me a clue, Alex."

"He was a U.S. general."

"Give me another clue, Alex."

"He was defeated at the Battle of Little Bighorn."

"One more clue, please."

"Um, his first name is George."

Mezmo ponders the historical personage until a timer buzzes. "Sorry, Mezmo," says Alex, "contestants are only allowed thirty seconds to answer each question."

"In that case I still have twenty-nine more seconds till my time runs out."

"Take your time, Mezmo," says Alex. "You still have twenty-nine seconds to go."

"I've got it!" says Mezmo, beaming with smug satisfaction.

"Would you like to share the answer with the rest of us?" says Alex.

"Sure," he says, pointing to the screen. "That is a photo of someone who is dead."

"You're on a roll, Mezmo!" says Alex, and the audience goes berserk with applause. "You know what this means don't you?"

"Of course I do. What does it mean?"

"This means it's time for *Double Difficulty!*" he says, flourishing his **a**rms hammily as though he were an orchestra conductor. "You know the rules, right?"

"Of course I do. I'm making them up as I go, but refresh my memory."

Alex recites the rules of the game without paying any attention to the words coming out of his mouth. He knows these rules better than he knows his own name, but only because Alex Winters is a lifetime away from little Alexei Andronavich. As a boy his secret name was Fear, and puberty transformed it to Doubt, then he matured to Desperation, and now, in his elder role, his secret name is Remorse, but the show must go on. Too cliché? That's Hollywood, deal with it. "You can choose to answer the *Double*

Difficulty question yourself or you can pass the question to one of the other contestants," he says absentmindedly, forgetting that Jacques is currently the only other contestant. "If you choose to answer the *Double Difficulty* question and you get it incorrect, your score goes down to zero and the other contestants, er, contestant, gets a chance to steal your points by answering the *Double Difficulty* question, but if you answer the question correctly, you'll get the chance to answer the *Maximum Difficulty* question for a million dollars, though if you fail to answer the million-dollar question, you'll feel shame for the rest of your life, and your wife and children will resent you, and you'll have to race Jacques against the buzzer on another *Double Difficulty* question, which means—

"Just get on with the game, Alex!"

"Does that mean you're ready to take the *Double Difficulty* challenge?"

"Yes already!"

"For the game, Mezmo—spell the word *Floccinauccinihilipilification*."

Mezmo looks like he just shit his pants. Even Alex doubts this word is real. "Could you use it in a sentence, Alex?"

"Sure thing, Mezmo. *Floccinauccinihilipilification* is the longest word in the first edition of the *Oxford English Dictionary*."

Alex isn't being insubordinate, or acting funny. He has no idea what the definition is. His teleprompter isn't feeding it to him.

"It would be a lot easier to answer the question if you told me how to spell it, Alex."

"That makes sense," says Alex, and he reads the letters off the teleprompter, "*F-l-o-c-c-i-n-a-u-c-c-i-n-i-h-i-l-i-p-i-l-i-f-i-c-a-t-i-o-n.*"

"That's my answer, Alex."

"Wow, Mezmo! You make it look so easy!" The audience gives him a standing ovation.

"And I sure do look handsome in my expensive Italian suit," says the Mentalist, staring directly into the camera.

"That suit looks really good on you, Mezmo!" says Alex. To be honest, Mezmo does look stylish in his three-button double-breasted charcoal gray Giorgio Armani made from hand-finished wool with Jacquard stitching. His hair looks fuller, lustrous, and his stomach appears to have deflated.

The fuzzy thud of Jacques Le Douche tapping on his microphone gets everyone's attention. "Are you sure Mezmo got the answer right, Alex?"

Mezmo is flabbergasted.

"What do you mean, Jacques?" says the game show host.

"I think he said *c-a-t*. That spells *cat*, not *floccinauccinihilipilification.*"

Alex Winters blushes from embarrassment. "You're absolutely right, Jacques."

"Hold on a minute!" says Mezmo. "What's going on here?"

"I won, and you're under arrest for conspiring to hypnotize approximately forty million viewers worldwide." He pulls a badge out of his pocket and holds it up for the cameras to see. "My name isn't really Jacques Le Douche." He grabs the top of his head and pulls his face off. It's a silicone mask. He is actually a she, and she's the spitting image of Lynda Carter from Wonder Woman. "I'm Special Agent Jacqueline Renifleur de Mégot of the Royal Canadian Psychic Surgery Prevention Unit." She stares deep into Mezmo's eyes. "Now go put some pants on."

Mezmo looks down and realizes he isn't wearing any pants, or underwear. The audience laughs at his pinky toe of a penis as he runs offstage.

Alex goes up to Jacqueline and shakes her hand. "Congratulations! You're our new *Maximum Difficulty* champion!"

"I knew it all along," says Wonder Woman, exuding total confidence.

— J. Martin Strangeweather

This hive-minded oddity owes its existence to the extraordinary imaginations of Tagert Ellis, J. G. McClure, Martina Hutchins, L. Joyce Morel, Justin Lee, Brennan Roach, Lance Boyle, and of course, Mr. F%!#@.

ABOUT THE CURATOR

J. Martin Strangeweather is a poet, a painter, a teller of tall tales, and the Chief Executive Prognosticator & Oneiric Director of Thaumaturgic Research for the Santa Ana Literary Association. He graduated from UC Irvine's renowned MFA program in English and Fiction, also earning degrees in Philosophy and Art History. Magister Strangeweather is the author of *Gorb in the Schizocratic Linguiverse,* published in June of 2018. *Gorb in the Schizocratic Linguiverse* is an intertextually self-aware experiment in alternative modes of narration, the literary equivalent of a psychotropic drug.